JOCK

A JOCK HARD NOVEL

RULE

USA TODAY BESTSELLING AUTHOR

SARA NEY

To Lexington.

You're what heroes are made of:
Tall. Strong. Masculine.
A bit flawed, a lot stubborn.
So good-looking (obviously).

Come *kiss* me already.

FIRST FRIDAY

"The Friday where I tell her she's a giant P word (and I don't mean Pretty)."

TEDDY

"Farmer Ted, can you do my makeup?"

I hate when my friend and roommate, Mariah, calls me Farmer Ted; she does it when she's trying to get my attention, and it always works.

But that doesn't mean I have to like it.

"Yeah, sure. I can do your makeup." Of course I can—I *always* do.

The foundation brush I'm holding between my fingers gets set on the counter, and instead of evening out my own complexion, I pull out a shade of concealer that matches Mariah's skin. Her skin is tan, thanks to copious amounts of fake bronzer, so I go with something dark, pulling a compact of bronzer from my drawer.

Mariah plops herself in a chair, closes her eyes, and tips her head back, waiting like she's a celebrity and I'm the stylist who has all the time in the world to work on her face.

I sigh.

If I do her makeup, I'm not going to have time to do mine. That fact doesn't escape my notice, but apparently it escapes hers.

Either that, or she just doesn't care.

"I'm thinking smoky eye," she murmurs, instructing me, not chatty other than to tell me what she wants.

It's fine; that's just how Mariah is—how she's always been.

"With a nude, glossy lip." She puckers her mouth, smacking her lips. Mariah is beautiful; I don't know why she feels it necessary to plump her lips and tan her skin and wear extensions.

I watch her watching herself in the mirror, and she glances at me over her shoulder, raising her dark brows. They're a stark contrast to her light-colored hair—almost too stark, but if I ever mentioned that to her, she'd get defensive.

"Shouldn't you be hurrying? We don't have tons of time."

I wouldn't call her *selfish*, but she is a little selfish.

Okay, fine—a lot selfish.

Love her to death, don't get me wrong, but even after all these years, Mariah Baker has always gotten what she's wanted, and I've always been the person to help her get it.

And right now, she wants me to do her makeup.

You can do this, Teddy. You can do Mariah's makeup first then crank out a quick blow-dry of your own hair, and once that's done, maybe even—

Mariah interrupts my musing. "Tessa and Cameron

want to meet a little earlier tonight. That's why we need to rush it. Are you down with that?"

Am I down with that?

I glance at the clock hanging on my bathroom wall, frowning. "When?" I still haven't done my hair. Or gotten dressed. "What time?"

"Nine. They heard there's a party at the rugby house."

Shit. That gives me no time to get myself ready.

"You want to party at the rugby house on the Row? That's so completely random." Usually it's the baseball or football houses my friends flock to; no one on campus gives a crap about rugby, and no one I know has ever dated a player.

It's not like any of these boys will play professionally—unlike the other sports—so it's kind of weird they have a designated house on Jock Row. At this university, living on "The Row" is the equivalent to being a king of campus: everyone wants to be an athlete, and everyone wants to date one.

It's the off-campus party scene, and students flock there every weekend.

"I've never heard of them having a party." I smudge black charcoal under Mariah's left eye. "Ever."

"Right, *but* they have some regional tournament or something coming up and they're throwing a blowout— it's supposed to be huge. Everyone will be there."

"Dang. *Every*one?" I drag out sarcastically, brushing shadow across her upper eyelid. "How big is their house?"

"Tiny." She's already eyeballing herself in the mirror, scrutinizing my work, pursing her lips. "It'll probably be in the backyard. If it sucks, we'll just ditch and go to a frat party."

"You don't think it's going to get out of hand, do you?"

Dark brows rise. "Why would it get out of hand?"

I stare back at her reflection in the mirror; the way she's watching has me feeling naïve and immature. "Uh... because they're rugby players and don't they usually fight a lot?" Not that I know anything about it, but I swear I heard somewhere they were kind of brutes, especially on the field.

Muddy, dirty brawlers.

Mariah shrugs. "God, Teddy, who cares if they fight a lot? A party is a party, and it's Friday night—what else is there to do?"

"*I* don't care. I was just *asking*." Why do I sound so defensive?

I swipe some blush across her cheekbones. Add highlighter. Do her eyebrows. Hand her the mascara wand.

"Here, go apply two thick coats."

"Just two?" She steals it from the tips of my fingers and stands, flouncing into my room to the mirror behind my bedroom door so she can get an up-close and personal look at what I've done to her eyes.

I swear, if we hadn't been best friends since we were seven, I'd wonder what the hell I was doing hanging out with her. Sometimes she's exhausting, and the older we get, the more opposite we become.

I catch a peek of myself in the mirror. Sigh with resignation, running my fingers through my long, brown hair— my stick-straight, *un*-styled hair. Stare at my wide brown eyes. My shiny skin, freshly scrubbed, complexion rosy—and also not bearing a speck of makeup.

Glance at the clock I hung in the bathroom so I wouldn't run late in the mornings before my eight o'clock class. 8:32. Mariah wants to leave by ten to nine, which gives me eighteen minutes to get completely ready.

Fuck my life.

***

"You can do this, Teddy. You're going to have a great time tonight."

God, why am I talking to myself in the mirror at a party?

It's because I've been hanging out alone since we got here, that's why, even though I've been in a room full of people.

I take a deep breath, checking my face one last time after washing my hands, no hand towel in sight. Using my jeans instead, I slide my palms up and down the denim, creating dark, damp streaks.

Someone bangs on the bathroom door.

"Just a minute!"

Startled, my lip gloss slips from my fingers to the dirty, laminate tile floor, and I cringe when the cap cracks. Pluck it off the disgusting floor like it's a flammable explosive.

"Dammit. This was my favorite," I complain to no one, fingertips barely grasping the tube as I toss the entire thing into the trash can, wash my hands again, and shoot myself one last cursory glance in the mirror before leaving the room.

I look good. Cute and natural.

Wearing way less makeup than I'd planned to when I had actual time to get myself ready, I lean against the water-soaked counter and sternly give myself another lecture.

"You're going to put yourself out there tonight. You're going to step outside your comfort zone and maybe you'll meet someone. No standing by the wall." I raise my brows at myself and point a finger at my reflection, unable to resist a pep talk. "No standing by the wall, you got it?"

I'm almost afraid to pull open the door, knowing a lynch mob is waiting on the other side—unhappy young women who had to stand in line while I screwed around inside the bathroom, giving myself a stern talking-to in the mirror.

My hand reaches for the doorknob. Unlocks it.

Clasps.

Pulls.

Loud music and voices assail me all at once, along with the line outside the door. I was right: some of them do look pissed off. Others lean on the wall for support, totally drunk. Not a surprise since this is a drinking party and everyone here is shit-faced.

Except for me.

Which reminds me...

I grab the red plastic cup off the counter, clutching it protectively in my hand as I nonchalantly breeze out the door as if nonplussed by the glaring, heavily made-up eyes.

Compared to them, I look like the girl next door.

I did what I could manage in the eighteen minutes Mariah left me to get ready, but it wasn't enough; I wasn't even able to do my hair. Thank God it's long, hanging in a flat, shiny sheet down over my shoulders, hiding the fact that my face barely has anything on it.

Concealer. Blush. A few swipes of sooty, black mascara. Nothing to write home about.

I look like the chaperone and not someone here for the party. Not even my outfit looks put together: black half boots, jeans, and a simple long-sleeved shirt I grabbed off the hanger in a rush.

It's not even cold outside yet.

I probably look ridiculous and out of place.

Lord knows I *feel* ridiculous.

Curse Mariah—she ditched me to play beer pong when I said I had to use the bathroom. Now I have to figure out where they're playing it…

"What were you doing in there, masturbating?" one of the girls in the hallway crudely asks as I squeeze past.

The rest of the line laughs.

I give the girls an awkward smile, shrugging my shoulders as if to say, *Sorry!* and slither away, head bent to find my friend.

The beer pong table where she said she'd be? Nowhere to be found.

I check the living room—nothing.

The kitchen. Back bedroom.

Ugh.

Slightly irritated, I gradually make my way to the backyard, where the crowd is gathered around a beer pong table I can hardly make out; the area is so congested it's almost impossible to move. I tiptoe down the porch steps, shielding my eyes from the blinding spotlight set up in the corner of the yard, and squint.

No sign of Mariah. Of course.

My breath hitches when I spy some familiar faces. Relieved, I push through the crowd, making a beeline for Tessa and Cameron, two girls we made friends with in the dorms our freshmen year. They've both always been really friendly, despite being jock chasers like—well, like Mariah.

God am I glad to see them.

It takes me a good ten minutes to claw my way to their side, and when I do, "Thank freaking God I spotted you. I was beginning to think I was going to spend the entire evening alone on the porch."

They give a collective squeal when they see me—of course they do, because they're *that* type of girl. Squealers. Always overexcited to see someone they saw the day before in the quad. Nevertheless, I let them hug me and fuss and act like we didn't walk to the party together tonight, like they haven't seen me in years.

"Teddy! Teddy, where have you been? We thought we lost you!" Tessa—blonde, beautiful Tessa—has eyes as wide as saucers and genuinely looks devastated by my disappearance.

That's what being drunk does to a person, I suppose.

She clutches my upper arm.

"I went to the bathroom and it took forever. Sorry," I shout over the noise, over the music blasting and everyone else who's trying to have a conversation and fight the climbing decibels.

They both nod knowingly. "Well you're back now."

Cam looks into my red cup. "But you're not drinking."

I was.

I tip the cup upside down. Empty. "I'm out."

"You can't have an empty cup—house rules."

I laugh. "It is not."

Cam's expression is somber as she bobs her head. "It is. That's what the kid at the keg told us."

"That's just something guys say so girls get drunk."

"But don't you want another beer?"

Not really. "Sure." I shrug. "I guess?"

"They moved the beer to the living room," Tessa informs me, though I passed it on my way to the backyard.

A keg in the living room—*classy*.

"Can you get us some, too, while you're in there?" Cam asks. "But get us new cups so we can keep drinking these." She holds up hers to demonstrate that it still has alcohol in it then gives the cup a shake in my direction. "Dumping this out to get new beer is alcohol abuse, even if it's super warm."

"I'll get you a new cup if they let me." We had to pay ten bucks at the door for a red plastic cup, and I hope they give me a new one without making me argue for it. Probably not, but it's worth a shot.

"They'll give you a new cup—you're adorable!" Cam enthuses, winking her heavily made-up eye. She really is a sweetheart, and I steal a glance at Tessa.

"If you see Mariah, tell her I'm looking for her?"

They both shrug, as if tied to marionette strings. "Sure."

"Thanks."

With that, I'm elbowing my way amidst the throng in the opposite direction I'd already struggled through—back over the yard, across the porch, into the kitchen.

"Excuse me…excuse me." It takes no less than fifteen minutes to reach the living room and the keg.

No one is manning it. No one is here to pump the hose thingy or whatever it's called.

No extra cups to be seen, not even on the floor. My eyes hit the floor, nose wrinkling at the soggy mess beneath the gray, metal keg. Beneath my feet.

Beer has spilled onto the floor, saturating the fibers of the already dirty carpet, squishing slightly when I shuffle my shoes. Gross.

Typical males, not having a sense of ownership and trashing the house they're lucky enough to live in, probably for half the rent I pay. I've never been that fortunate; I have to work for everything I have, including tuition, because my mom can't afford to help me, not even while working two jobs, one as a bartender and waitress in the tourist town we live in.

It sucks, but I've never had handouts. I've never known anything but hard work, so seeing this house being trashed so carelessly…

I swallow.

It's none of my business what these guys do. I'm only here for beer and to hang out with my friends, and why the heck do I even care? Let them ruin their stupid carpet! It doesn't affect me one bit.

***

KIP

That girl has been standing next to the keg for way too long.

I should probably go tell her it's tapped, completely out of beer, and we're just waiting for someone to come pick the damn thing up, but...

I won't.

Instead, I lean against the wall and take a long pull from the beer I brought that's locked in the fridge at the back of the house.

She glances from side to side, waiting with her red cup, shifting on her heels, grimacing at her feet every so often, a completely disgusted look on her face.

It's a pretty face.

If you're into pure and perfect and barely made-up.

Which I'm not.

I'm not into any faces, hot or cute or not.

I don't date. I don't have sex, don't get involved with anyone.

But.

The girl is cute in a clueless way, and I'm compelled to study her as she stands there, waiting for beer.

The house is packed—we knew it would be—the entire student body seemingly crammed into our living room, busting out onto the porch, into the yard, and even into the unfinished basement. It's nothing but cinder block and musty smells, but it's packed full of drunken idiots.

I cringe when the curtains at the far side of the room

come crashing down then wait for the aftermath: loud laughter and cackling. The dude who made the mess wraps himself up, fashioning a toga, curtain rod and all, loudly proclaiming himself emperor of the party.

Fucking moron.

The cold amber bottle in my hand touches my lips as my eyes casually slide back to the waiter. Still standing in the center of the room looking aimless. Unsure. Self-conscious.

She tucks a long strand of brown hair behind her ear and bites down on her lower lip, nibbling. Readjusts her weight.

Why hasn't she given up yet and gone hunting around for another keg? It's on the freaking front porch; anyone with half a brain would have given up and gone searching.

Not this chick.

She's rooted to the floor like it's her fucking job to stand in that one spot.

Another swig from my bottle has me settling against the wall behind me, my massive shoulder slouched against the drywall. Bored.

At six foot four, I have a bird's-eye view of the entire living room. I'm a head taller than most people here, definitely taller than all the chicks. A few of my teammates come close to my height, but not many.

Brawny.

My scowl keeps the girls at bay, and I arch my brows when an errant female partygoer mistakes me for someone who wants to talk.

I don't.

Not to her.

And not to the blonde in the low-cut black dress. Or the one in the midriff-baring top and low-rise jeans. Or the one flipping her hair in ten different directions as she looks me up and down, blue gaze landing on my junk.

Jesus, these girls.

No class. No shame.

I have one semester and summer classes left before I can go through commencement; I'm not going to spend the time chained to some needy cleat chaser or a gold digger who's only after my family's money.

Not even one as pretty as the girl in the middle of the room.

I don't know why I'm freaking staring at her. She's not "hot," or drunk, or the type that typically shows up when we have parties.

She looks more conservative, self-conscious and…out of place.

Long, straight hair. Black shirt. Jeans. Barely any makeup from what I can see from here, and she's pushed the strands of her hair away from her face no less than four times already.

Yup, I'm counting.

Watching as Smith Jackson approaches her, I barely contain an eye roll when his blaring smile aims in her direction as he swipes one of his tan hands through his jet black hair.

Flirting.

Smith is on the soccer team and a giant douchebag.

Does hard drugs recreationally—shit like coke. Treats

girls like crap, from what I've heard. Takes advantage of the services offered to athletes, like preferred class selection, then skips those classes.

Basically, Smith Jackson is a real cunt.

I have no fucking idea why girls drop their panties for him.

Oh—yeah I do: he's an athlete and he's good-looking. But who the fuck names their kid Smith? Who?

He's sizing up the girl by the keg, but with a familiar air surrounding the approach that makes me think they've met. He taps her on the elbow. Smiles again. She nods.

Yup, they definitely know each other from somewhere. Class maybe? Definitely haven't fucked or he never would have approached her; he's not the double-dipping type, not from what I've seen.

The kid is well and truly a total dipshit.

I lean back, get comfortable, and watch.

The girl isn't bothered by him or overly charmed, but she's blushing—I can see the tint on her cheeks from here, damn near across the room, and I can see the brightness of her face. Her high cheekbones shine. Her teeth are white and blinding.

She's nervous but trying to be nonchalant, as if she gets approached all the time, when it's obvious to me that she doesn't.

I wonder what Smith wants from her. Why he walked over.

He grabs the hose to the keg and holds it up, demonstrating to her that it's tapped out.

"See?" He laughs, tipping his head back. Mocking her

a little until her head bows a bit.

Fucker.

He gives her a nudge, dropping the black line to the beer. It falls to the carpet and he sets it on the metal barrel, crossing his arms and looking up at her. Puppy dog eyes? *Really*, Smith?

I can't see the girl's face anymore—just her back and the long brown hair spilling down it—but her arms eventually come uncrossed and her posture relaxes. Whatever it is Smith is saying, it's easing her tension. It's probably garbage, but she seems comfortable.

And another one bites the dust.

They always fall for his shit.

Content to watch the party from the corner of the room, I slouch so I'm not standing at my full height, scratching at the full beard growing on my face. It's been about two years since I shaved the hair on my chin, cheeks, and jawline, and I have no intention of doing so any time soon.

I wouldn't call it bushy, but it's pretty damn close. Unkempt. Scratchy.

My mother hates it. My sister hates it.

Girls on campus hate it.

The beard serves its purpose perfectly.

Despite my size, build, and status on campus, I'm left alone all night. Not a single female approaches me, if you don't count the girls in the kitchen who needed cups taken down off the top of the fridge earlier in the evening.

The mop of man bun on top of my head wobbles when I give it an agitated toss. For a hot minute, when I first transferred to Iowa, I'd actually thought about living in this dump.

Fortunately, I learned a few general rules quickly enough from spending time with my teammates:

1. Nothing is sacred if you're a member of the team, so anyone living here better get a goddamn lock on their bedroom door.
2. It's loud every damn weekend, whether a party is happening or not.
3. Guys are slobs when there is no one cleaning up after them. And no one is.
4. Even with a lock on your bedroom door, there is still no peace in this place.
5. Everyone is in everyone's business.

Whatever.

Anyway.

I swipe at the hair in my eyes.

Bend at the waist, setting my half-empty beer bottle on the ground, resting it between my feet so it doesn't spill. Pull the rubber band out of my hair and shake my entire head, dipping over to gather it in my hands. Yank it into a top knot and wrap the black elastic band around it.

"Looking good, Sasquatch. You really shouldn't have gotten all fancy for us," one of my teammates goads from a few feet away, having caught me doing my hair. "Want to blow me later?"

My hands are now free, so I flip him off. "Fuck the fuck off, Winkowski."

"But you're such a pretty girl."

Yeah, yeah, yeah. Ha ha. Jesus, these guys. Constantly giving me shit about my appearance—as if I give a crap what they think about my hair. Nothing I haven't been hearing the two years since I decided to let it all grow out.

It's easier this way.

Less distraction.

Less of a pain in the ass.

The hair and the beard work because I'm not getting approached constantly, and no girls are trying to get themselves knocked up.

I'm no one's sugar daddy and no chick's meal ticket.

So, here's the thing: my parents are…wealthy. And not the millionaire-next-door kind of rich. No. They're the *You want to have dinner in Vegas tonight? Let's take the leer jet.* kind of rich. Hilton rich. Rockefeller rich.

Sometimes it blows dick that Dad is one of the biggest employers in the state and owns one of the largest manufacturing plants in the country, located right here in Iowa. It's like wearing a big, red target on my back, and eventually…I got sick and tired of it.

Don't get me wrong—I love them like crazy. Our family is really close. But along with my parents, come the *people*; the assistants. The users. The ass-kissing employees.

It was time to distance myself from it all, at least for the time being—while I have the chance.

My sister got to change her last name when she got married; she didn't even hyphenate like most socialites tend to do. Nope. Not Veronica. Lost the Carmichael name entirely, moved to Bumblefuck, USA, and only comes back for the holidays and big charity events—and even then, she digs her heels in.

Stiletto heels, but still.

My sister has a giant set of lady balls, and I'm trying to follow in her footsteps by becoming my own man—not the obedient scion my father expects me to be.

So.

The first middle finger to my lifestyle was me dropping out of Notre Dame—Dad's alma mater—after one year and transferring to Iowa.

My parents have actually been pretty damn cool about it, albeit a little uptight from lack of understanding. They're really regimented from habit and set in their ways, getting everything and anything they want. Their expectations of people can be ridiculous and often times impossible to meet. But, they worked their asses off to get where they are, building a company—actually, an empire—over the course of thirty years.

You get the picture; I don't have to paint it for you.

The point is: I do what I want.

And when the time comes, when I feel ready, I'll take my place at my dad's company—and not a day before.

I asserted my independence and hid out, growing out my hair and beard and not giving a shit what I looked like.

Sometimes, no matter how rich a guy is, girls just aren't willing to put up with all the unruly hair.

It's the perfect fucking disguise.

Genius, really.

Smith Jackson is a trust fund baby too. Not like I am, of course—very few people are—but the difference between us is that I'm not a self-centered, narcissistic prick. I'm no shrink and haven't diagnosed him, but because of how I grew up, I know a self-serving asshole when I meet one.

Jesus, I don't even know why I'm bothering to think about it, but any time I see him with a girl, it makes the hairs on the back of my neck stand up.

The girl seems to be warming up to him, slowly but surely, her shoulders relaxing in a way they weren't when he first walked up. Her laugh looks like it's coming easier, less forced. She's not touching her face anymore or fidgeting with her long hair.

I watch.

I watch as three more girls approach, shouldering their way into the conversation, the one with dark hair planting herself firmly in front of Smith. Flipping her hair and laughing so loud I can hear it from here, and believe me— nothing that jackass is saying could possibly be that funny.

There is no fucking way.

The blonde one in the group throws her arm over the quiet girl's shoulders. Gives it a squeeze.

Ah, so they know her.

She gives a weak smile, her eyes darting to Smith, that smile eventually fading until it's nothing but a flat line of confusion. Resignation.

I see her body sigh, and she's back to brushing her hair to the side, out of her pretty face.

Smith touches one of the friends, fingering the strap of her skimpy tank top, earning himself yet another loud, fake laugh. He smiles.

She smiles, and…

I'm instantly irritated.

Her friends are jock-blocking—so fucking typical. I recognize their type: jersey chasers. Gold diggers. Here for the MRS degree and not for an actual education because there are so many athletes running around this university who will end up in the pros.

And these girls reek of desperation: while their pretty, shy friend was chatting Jackson up, instead of leaving her to it and letting her enjoy the moment, they swoop in and flirt with him instead. Like vultures. How fucking shitty is that?

I've seen it over and over and over, and it pisses me off every fucking time. Why are chicks like this? Why are they such backstabbing *bit*ches?

I can't hide my scowl.

That right there is the reason for the long hair and the beard, and for the *I gave up giving a shit* attitude toward women. That right there.

No loyalty with these girls when they see something they want.

Man, if I had friends like that, I'd want to fucking cut my own balls off with a dull knife.

That's not true—I wouldn't let anyone near my nuts with a dull knife, let alone have the fucking nerve to hack them off myself.

I lift the beer bottle in my hand and take a healthy swig. Wipe at the liquid dripping from the corner of my mouth with a wry smile.

SECOND FRIDAY

"The Friday where she learns she needs a bigger set of lady balls."

KIP

She's back.

And this time, she's dolled herself up a bit more.

No, not a bit more—a *lot* more.

Her long hair that was straight last week falls in waves down her back. Last week it looked like her eyes were free of makeup, now they're coated with mascara and dark eye shadow. Full, pink, shiny lips. Large, gold hoop earrings hang from her ears.

The girl is wearing a yellow sundress, sticking out like a goddamn sore thumb in this room full of provocative clothing. It's got thick straps that are tied around the back of her neck in a bow, the waist snug and skirt flaring out around her hips.

The outfit is conservative and sweet, and I almost feel bad for her.

She's on the taller side with toned, tan arms and a tentative smile curving just above the rim of her red beer cup. Eyes roam around the room but don't make it as far as my spot in the corner—the same spot I stood in last weekend, silently judging everyone in the room.

I sigh.

This is fucking boring.

I don't understand why these assholes keep having parties; it's not like anyone gives two shits about rugby at this school—they reserve the top spots on the totem for wrestling, football, and baseball. I don't give a shit, but if our captains keep throwing keggers, someone at campus security is going to notice and nail us, and we won't be able to talk our way out of any fines.

Not like the assholes in the other houses can. And do.

Trust me, I've seen squad cars come and go plenty, but they never linger out front for long.

Lucky fucks.

Entitled.

I snort. Like I'm one to talk. Life at home doesn't get any more privileged than I have it, but at least I'm not a total prick when I'm out in public, or to anyone living in the house. For all they know, my father is a mechanic and my mom is a school secretary. None of them have a clue because guys do not give a crap about that kind of thing.

If any of them found out, I'd probably catch a rash of shit for it.

Girls, on the other hand…

The less they know, the better. And the only way to keep someone at arm's length is to not get involved.

Easy.

I've managed for the past two years, and I'll manage until I graduate in the winter.

Speaking of girls...

I can't believe what I'm seeing: the chick from last weekend is down by the keg—again—and has been filling beer cups in the middle of the room for the past hour. Every so often that dark-haired friend of hers wanders over, flirting and talking to whatever guy the girl is chatting with—then walk off with him.

Cockblocking harpie.

I watch as Phil Blaser, a rookie hooker on the rugby team, saunters off, confident that the girl has the whole thing handled—a job he's supposed to perform the entire night.

Why the fuck is Phil leaving, and what the actual fuck does she think she's doing filling beer cups?

Wow. This girl.

She is *way* too polite—it's almost painful to watch. Jesus, she needs help, and not the kind a shrink can provide; no dude, she needs a reality check. This is the second weekend in a row I watch her get taken advantage of—not an attractive quality. First by her friends—a trio of jock-strap-pursuing jersey chasers—then tonight by Phil, a member of my team.

I make a mental note to find him, wring his scrawny neck, and lecture him about treating women with more respect. This is our house—it's his goddamn job to stand rooted in that spot and keep our guests happy, not hers. We fucking assigned him that spot. Then he hands the hose off to some girl?

What the actual fuck, Phil?

Not only that, it's the same girl as last weekend—a girl who obviously needs to be taught how to say, *Go screw yourselves and stop walking all over me.*

That's a bit of brutal honesty she'll only get from someone who couldn't care less about her feelings.

Someone like me.

***

TEDDY

I've been standing in this same spot for over an hour.

At first, it was because I had to get in line for the keg, then, when they kid at the tap finally handed me the hose to fill my own glass...

Somehow, I never let it go.

Or. No one took it from me?

Somehow, without my noticing, a giant of a man-child sidles up to me, shadow looming from above, almost blocking the light.

That's how large he is.

That's how large he seems, anyway.

Gingerly, without speaking, he plucks the tap hose out of my grip, grasping the nozzle in a giant hand, pinching it between two fingers and holding it over his cup. The hose hisses from having air in the line, so the big dude reaches down and gives the barrel a few pumps.

Holds the nozzle down again. Fills his cup without speaking to me.

Then, "Where's your tip jar?" He's still not looking at me, intent on watching the foam building over his beer.

Flicks the top off onto the rug beneath the keg before meeting my eyes.

His are big, brown, and framed by arched bushy brows, a hair-covered face, neck, and head.

His whole appearance is startling. He's kind of a mix between Wolverine, Teen Wolf, and Bigfoot—if Bigfoot were real. And now he's pinning me to the floor with his question.

"Excuse me?"

"Don't all bartenders have a tip jar?"

"I'm not the bartender." Did he really think I was? I can't for the life of me read his expression under that bush.

"I know that. I was fucking with you."

"Oh." Yeah, I said *Oh*, as if it was the best response I could come up with. Then, because I'm a genius, I follow it up with, "*Why?*"

"Because you're just standing here filling everyone's cups like a fucking bartender, that's why."

It's on the tip of my tongue to squeak out a loud, *I am not!*

My lips part to protest, but the words won't come out because…my god, he's right—I *have* been standing here filling cups. I don't even know for how long. How did that happen? It's kind of like holding a door for someone at the store. You do it for one person then more come, and before you know it, you're stuck standing there.

I wasn't doing it on *pur*pose, and this guy?

He noticed.

I glance around, wondering if anyone else did too.

Shit. How embarrassing.

"Why do you keep coming back if you're just going to stand here all night?"

"What do you mean, keep coming back?"

"Last weekend you did the same thing—walked over to the keg and stood there."

"I did?"

"Yes."

Who the hell is this guy?

"How do you know? Were you watching me?"

His broad shoulders shrug—no, not broad. Mammoth. *Wide.* Expansive. All better words to describe the width of this guy's amazing upper body.

I avert my curious gaze.

This guy is freaking huge, his intelligent, intense gaze following mine across the room curiously when they land on some guy with shocking red hair near the kitchen wearing a bright blue polo shirt. "You like Jasper Winters?"

"Who?" My palms are sweating, making the cup in my hand slippery. "I don't even know him."

He rolls his eyes. "Do you want to know him—like, biblically?"

"What? No! *Jeez,* all I did was look in his direction. Would you stop?" *What is with this dude?* I try to steer the conversation. "And how do you know I was standing by the keg last weekend?"

Those bright, caramel colored brown eyes bore into me. Roll. "I saw you."

It's my turn to roll my eyes. "Well no shit. But why?"

"I was holding up the wall over there, and it was hard not to notice when you didn't move the entire night. You know"—he tips his cup in my direction—"kind of like you're doing right now." He finally lets the hose from the keg drop to the floor. "There. Now you're officially off duty—let them pour their own fucking beer."

His voice has a timbre so low, my cheeks flush to the point I'm tempted to cool them with the palms of my hands. It's deep and masculine and—

"Rule one: if you're going to date one of these guys, you can't be a pussy."

I'm sorry, did he just say…the *P* word?

Now I'm blushing for an entirely different reason. He could have chosen any other word in the dictionary but that one. Wuss. Chicken. Wimp.

But no. He went with *pussy* and made my cheeks flush so fast I can feel the blood flow hit my face.

"*Excuse* me?"

"Don't be a pussy," he repeats casually, taking a deep chug of the beer inside his red cup.

"I…I… Who says I want to date one of"—my hands flail through the air helplessly as I choke on the rest of my words—"these guys?"

He takes another chug. Another swallow.

Raises a thick brow. "Don't you?"

My hands smooth down the front pleats of my yellow skirt and when I look up, I notice his eyes tracking my fingers.

"No! I mean, not these guys specifically." And not just any guy. A gentleman—someone smart, who can make me laugh and have a good time. Someone on a career track so I—we—never have to struggle financially—like my Mom always had to after my dad walked out on her. Us.

Someone—

"Uh…hello?"

He says it in that tone you reserve for your idiot friends who can't take a hint or don't have a clue.

Nice.

Our eyes connect when I look up. He's so tall I have to stretch my neck and tilt my head back to meet his gaze.

This guy. How do I describe him?

Crude. He's already said pussy twice, and the set of his lips is sarcastic, even if no words are coming out of them at the moment.

He's a giant, taller than anyone else in the room—or anyone I've ever met for that matter. Six three? Six five?

Definitely too hairy.

My eyes rake down his chest—his shirt is actually nice, looks expensive, despite the droplets of beer soaking in beneath the logo on his right pec. His hair is dirty blond and long, pulled up into a topknot—much like the one I wear when I'm in a rush and have no time to do my hair, only his is messier.

He has a mustache and beard too—not one of those neatly groomed, manscaped ones that are so trendy right now.

No.

His is…unkempt, untrimmed, burly. Kind of pre-mountain man meets college hobo meets mass murderer in training. I've never seen a beard like this on a college kid. Once, in high school, there was this wrestler with one, a big, burly, farm kid who gave zero shits about what anyone thought. He did what he wanted, including sporting a beard, which I don't think was allowed. He looked older than most of the faculty.

The thought makes me smile. Shit, what was his name... Mitch? Darren?

"Hi." His deep voice snaps me out of my perusal. "My eyes are up here."

Somewhere is a mouth—one I faintly detect. *Somewhere*, I want to sass, *shadowed by one of the most ridiculous mustaches I've ever seen on a grown man.* Can barely tell if his lips are tipped into a smile or in a straight, serious line. It's impossible to be sure if he's joking or not.

I lift my chin and study him. Unwavering eyes. Purposeful gaze, unflinching. Straight brows.

Oh.

Crap, he *isn't* kidding—I think it's seriously bothering him that I'm checking out his body.

"I'm sorry. I wasn't staring." I mean, I was, but not to be rude. Merely curious.

What was his original point? Pussy—god, that word—and something about rules and dating and the guys in this place?

Beards.

Jesus, my eyes are straying again and I swear I'm not doing it on purpose—there is just too much to see. His large brown eyes, the bushy brows. The man bun, the beard.

This guy is so freaking...

Hairy.

And intense.

I give my head a physical shake. "I'm sorry, what were you saying?"

He expels a loud sigh. "We were talking about how if you're going to date one of the guys here, you can't be such a goddamn pussy."

"No we weren't. I never said anything about dating guys *here*—you did."

He snorts then takes a drag from the cup in his hand. "Please. Everyone wants to date the guys around here."

"Rugby players?" I scoff, disguising my snort with a cough. "I don't think so."

"Rugby players isn't what I meant—I meant athletes at this school in general." He lifts a leg, propping his massive booted foot on top of the metal keg. "But what's wrong with rugby players?"

"Nothing!" I don't want to offend him, it's just... "Nothing is wrong with them, but I don't think they're any girl's first choice in the hierarchy."

That sounded so rude, the candor surprising me, and I clamp a hand over my lips to shut myself up.

I shouldn't have any more beer.

"Well even if that's not the case, you are without a doubt the worst jersey chaser I've ever seen—and I've seen shit tons of them come through these parties. You're terrible."

"Did you just call me a...a..." I can't even get the words out.

"Jersey chaser? Yeah. You didn't hear me stutter, did you?"

"What would make you say that?" I'm one second away from clutching a hand to my chest at the indignation of it all.

"Dude, you've been here *two* weekends in a row, chatting up everyone and standing next to the keg—that's prime real estate. That's where all the guys congregate."

Is it? I guess I hadn't noticed.

"I did not do that on p-purpose!" I'm sputtering. Actually sputtering.

The giant takes another long pull from his cup. Swallows, his Adam's apple somewhere in his throat concealed by all the hair. He's in desperate need of a shave but clearly does not give a shit.

"Whatever you say, jersey chaser." His drawl is nonchalant, and it's obvious he doesn't believe me.

"I don't!" Wait, that didn't make sense. "I'm not!"

Those wide, lumberjack shoulders shrug. "Whatever you say."

"Stop doing that."

"Doing what?"

"Agreeing with me in a patronizing manner." God do I sound like a prig.

One of his dark brows rises. "A patronizing manner? What the fuck is that? It sounds exactly like something my *mom* would say."

Could this conversation get any worse?

"Look, *man.*" The word comes out of my mouth before I can stop it, further adding to my stuffy demeanor, but honestly, I have no idea what to say. "Thanks for the advice, but I don't think I need it." *Especially not from someone who looks like he just emerged from the wilderness after being lost for a month.*

"Just trying to help."

"I don't need help."

His shoulders hunch as he laughs, and they shake a little with the action. "Sure you don't."

Pretty sure I'm gaping, mouth wide open. "I don't! And I wasn't trying to flirt with anyone so—whatever!"

"Then you were doing a great job." His mustache twitches. "Until your friends showed up."

Okay. Now he has my full attention, and I jut out a hip. "What about my friends?"

"They're cock-blockers."

Huh? "No they're not."

"So you weren't flirting with Smith Jackson, and tonight you weren't flirting with Ben Thompson, and your dark-haired friend didn't come up and steal them both away?"

Wait...*what?* How does he know all this? "Smith Jackson who?"

I have no idea which guy he's talking about, but they've all been nice. And so what if they've all walked off with Mariah? I wasn't interested in them anyway.

"Were you watching me last week too?"

He shrugs. "Yes."

His honestly confuses me. Most guys would lie or make up a lame excuse. "Why?"

"I had nothing better to do."

Well then. "And you don't think that's strange?"

"Nope—not when you're bored." The guy snorts through the hair growing under his Grecian nose. "It's not like I'm interested in you."

Wow. "Gee, thanks."

"No offense." He looks like he couldn't care less if he's insulted me.

"None taken?"

He laughs again. "You sure about that? Now you look kind of pissed."

Not pissed—but slightly offended. And embarrassed. And confused.

"Listen, I'm not trying to be a dick, okay? But you can't come into a house like this and act like a deer caught in headlights. That just makes you an easy target. And if you're interested in someone, you can't stand there when one of your idiot friends hits on him and do nothing about it." His voice is a baritone and drones on, doling out more unsolicited advice. "You can't let your friends walk all over you."

What the hell is he talking about? "I don't!"

A pair of chocolate brown eyes settle toward the ceiling. "You're in total denial. Your dark-haired friend is a total asshole—the female equivalent of a douchebag."

Is he talking about Mariah? "Okay, this conversation is over."

"Whatever. Suit yourself."

"I'm walking away now." My feet stay rooted to the spot.

The guy smirks…I think—it's hard to tell with all the hair covering his mouth, but a set of straight, pearly white teeth flash, causing me to blink upward.

And now I'm staring again.

"Go. Don't let me stop you." I swear, he keeps taking sips of his beer for dramatic flare, flawlessly timed pauses. "Have fun."

Annoying.

"I will."

"I'm sure you will."

"I will." Why am I arguing with this guy? Jeez, Teddy, stop repeating yourself or he'll think you're a moron. Not true, I continue protesting to myself, because he already does. Thinks he's so damn smart, watching everyone from the corner like a creeper. Judging.

Mariah is not a cock-blocker! She would never…

Besides, I scoff, it's not like I wanted any of those guys to hit on me—we were just talking. I was standing at the keg, and they came up for beer, not to hit on me. And I certainly would never hit on a guy—not on purpose, anyway.

If Mariah, Cameron, and Tessa happened to come up at that exact same time and join the chat, and Mariah just happened to have better chemistry with someone, that has nothing at all to do with me.

She would *never* purposely…

I feel my brow tighten and furrow, glancing at my feet, at the open-toed, brown leather wedges buckled around my ankles. Cute. Pretty.

Sunk into the worn, stained carpet that's been beat to hell from all the abuse, still standing in the spot I just declared I was walking away from.

My gaze wanders, settling on those stupid work boots.

Who wears that kind of footwear these days? Seriously? Lumberjacks, construction workers, and bad male rappers, that's who, not twenty-something-year-old college guys at a house party. What is he even doing?

My lips purse with annoyance.

My eyes slide up his denim-clad legs, quickly passing over the slight bulge of his crotch—he doesn't have a hard-on, but since I know he has a dick in his pants, naturally I want to look. Narrow waist. Belt. T-shirt half tucked at his hips.

Broad chest.

"Hey, look at you, leaving and shit. Good job following through." With one hand clasped around his red cup, he smacks it with the other in a mock clap, holding it forward so it doesn't spill.

My god, could he embarrass me any more?

"Your friends went that way." He points, the mammoth paw at the end of his hairy arm raised and directed toward the back of the house.

"Thanks."

"No prob—I'm here to help."

"Is that what you're doing? Helping?"

"I do what I can."

I cross my arms over my breasts, mindful that my cleavage is now plumped and uncomfortably on display. I immediately uncross them—from his bird's-eye view, no doubt he can see right down the valley between my boobs. "I didn't ask for you to give me advice or stalk my friends or cast judgment on me."

"Then you shouldn't make it so damn easy." He has the

nerve to laugh, tipping back his beard-covered neck. The stubble is thick and dark blond, and I want to pull on it to get him to stop talking.

A few deeps breaths and I've sorted my insides out, quelling the unease that has been growing in the pit of my stomach. I smooth a hand over my abs, down the pleats in my pretty yellow sundress—a nervous habit I've caught myself doing on more than one occasion.

Expel a long, drawn-out breath he won't be able to hear above the noise.

"It was nice meeting you."

Only it wasn't, because we didn't actually meet. I have no idea what his name is, where he's from, what his deal is.

He tilts his head. "Same."

"*Bye.*"

When I chance a glance over my shoulder, the behemoth is watching, cup to his lips. It's paused there, suspended, dark eyes boring into me.

Wow. He really is freaking huge. And honestly, not polite and not at all cute.

With a grimace, I give my head a shake and keep walking.

THIRD FRIDAY

"The Friday where he's a combination of Neanderthal and Prince Charming."

TEDDY

This is the third weekend in a row we've been at the rugby house, and I don't have any solid proof, but I'm almost positive Mariah is hooking up with one of them. She hasn't said anything to me about it, but why else would we keep coming back? She either likes someone here or she's already sleeping with them.

I fiddle with the cup in my hand, conscious of the fact that once again, I've been left alone to fend for myself while my childhood friend works the room, having ditched me within minutes of our arrival.

It stings a little, if I'm being honest.

I wouldn't have come tonight if I had known she was going to once again leave me hanging.

She never used to be like this; in high school, we were inseparable. When we began applying to colleges, against her parents' and my mom's better judgment, we applied to all the same schools. Lived together in the dorms our freshmen and sophomore years. Now, it's our junior year.

We used to be attached at the hip, and now it seems I've become a second thought where Mariah is concerned.

In any case, I'm not going to get stuck standing by the keg tonight and risk the chance of being caught by that... that...

Guy.

He weirds me out, not because he's creepy or perverted, but because he's way too honest, and it makes me uncomfortable. Don't get me wrong, I don't need to have things sugarcoated, but he did bring up a subject that's been on my mind a lot lately and that I've been a bit salty about.

Mariah taking advantage of our friendship. Of me.

The fact that a complete stranger picked up on it is embarrassing. I'd like to avoid him if humanly possible. Tonight, I want to have fun, not have it thrown in my face that my friends keep throwing me over for boys.

I move along the perimeter of the room, putting up the pretense that I'm not scanning the room for him.

Him.

That guy—whatever his name is.

I wonder about that as I grip the cold red cup in my hand. Try to picture what a guy like that could possibly be named.

What would I name a lumberjack baby if I had one?

Billy Ray. John Boy? Duane.

Cooter—that one makes me laugh, and I choke on the foam rimming my cup. The name Woody makes me laugh too, and by the time I look up and meet his eyes, I'm almost stupid giddy.

He's scowling at me, of course, and wearing a plaid flannel shirt, sleeves rolled and pushed to the elbow.

His hair is up, twisted into a messy mop, long strands escaping at his temples, curling up and around his ears. It's a gorgeous dirty blond, naturally streaked from the sun, a hue any girl would kill for and few could recreate.

Skin tan, high cheekbones pink. Not ruddy, but close.

The beard still long, although from here, it does look like he might have cleaned it up a bit? I have no interest in finding out—the last thing I want is for him to come over.

God no.

I rotate my body, presenting him with my back, and come face to face with the keg.

Dammit.

Move to the side a few feet, creating more distance between us, not sure what to do with myself because once again, I'm standing in the middle of a party alone.

I should be pissed at my friends, but the truth is, I'm relieved; standing with them is too much pressure. Too many people coming up to chat, too many guys coming up to flirt. Drunk guys make me nervous. Guys who are hitting on us make me nervous.

Drunk guys who are hitting on us make me nervous.

Unfortunately, that's what I'm surrounded by, and unfortunately, I've been left to fend for myself.

The party is packed—third weekend in a row. I make a silent vow not to return for a fourth, not if I can help it. I'm bored and, stifling a yawn, take a drag of my beer for lack of anything better to do.

Stop watching me, I implore the hairy guy, still feeling his eyes on the back of my head.

The skin on my neck prickles.

Stop it. I'm not turning around.

My nose twitches despite itself, my head gives a little shake.

No.

Jeez. Doesn't he have anything better to do other than stand there and creep on people who want to be left alone? I mean, not that I'm alone, alone. We are, after all, in a room full of people.

My gaze wanders.

Is he still looking? I'm dying to look over my shoulder but square them instead, standing taller on the heels of my tall, brown boots. Tap a toe impatiently, craning my head to survey the room.

If I tilt it just so, maybe I can catch a glimpse of him out of the corner of my eye without actually having to turn my head? I test the theory, adding a hand to the column of my neck, faux-massaging it, lifting my cup to my lips.

So smooth.

Shift my eyes to the right.

Heart plummeting to my stomach because those sullen brown eyes of his are indeed locked on my short frame. I'm not facing him, but they're so bright and striking I can make them out nonetheless. Even shrouded amongst all that hair.

Is he judging me? He must be—why else would he be attempting to telekinetically drill holes into the back of my skull? No doubt he thinks I'm a loser with no friends.

No—he thinks I'm a loser with *shitty* friends.

Big difference.

He doesn't like them and doesn't even know them. Or me, for that matter.

Judgy, arrogant asshole.

My throat *hmphs* indignantly.

A noise from the kitchen has my head jerking in that general direction. Two huge guys spill through the narrow door and into the living room. It looks like they're fighting—or wrestling?

I recognize one of the moves as a half nelson, and the entire scene suddenly escalates when one of the guys maneuvers his meaty right arm, hooks it around the others guy's neck, and pulls the guy down. Down onto the dirty, disgusting shag carpet.

Gross.

They're both grunting, feet smashing into end tables. The wall.

One booted foot kicks. Entire body thrashes.

The guy on the bottom is unsuccessfully trying to untangle himself from whatever hold he's in now, floundering like a fish out of water. Flopping, too drunk to remove himself but giving it the old college try.

Face bright red, he's sputtering, getting pissed.

Steam practically rolls out of his nostrils as he throws his head back, trying to knock it against his opponent's sweaty forehead.

No luck.

"Fuck you, Kissinger," he slurs. "Let me the fuck up."

Kissinger laughs, squeezing his arms like a python, wrapping them tighter.

The crowd shifts, girls gasping, people calling out. Cheering. Stumbling around, trying to make room as the boys tussle.

An elbow is released, nailing Kissinger in the gut. It's not a taut stomach; he clearly hasn't missed a kegger in months, beer belly pronounced.

A punch.

Someone gets kicked and falls over as blood gushes from his nose.

Girls scream—so dramatic—and a few guys on the perimeter of the room start shoving people forward, toward the fight. Why? I have no idea, but it creates chaos and more fists are thrown, this time from spectators, not the two dudes still on the floor.

The person closest to me stumbles backward, and I take a step back to prevent myself from getting jostled. Another and another and my back is almost pressed firmly against the wall, eyes bugging out when half the room erupts into right hooks and punches.

"Oh my god," I say breathlessly as I exhale, the scene playing out in front of me a far cry from how the evening began.

I measure the distance to the front door, the bodies in my way. The noise. The chanting and cheering from the idiots watching instead of breaking up the brawls.

A large hand cuffs my arm and I barely have time to look down before I'm being ushered toward the exit, full cup of beer still clutched in my hand.

When that warm hand leaves my bicep and juts out,

clearing the way, I have time to glance over my shoulder for a look at my rescuer.

The hairy guy whose name I haven't figured out yet.

Roy?

Paul Bunyan without the ox. Without the axe.

Rescuing me.

But why?

I whip around, an errant elbow slamming into my body, sending me lurching forward—backward? I don't know. I can't stand straight and would have hit the wall if not for…

My beer cup goes soaring; his does too, splashing down the front of my dress. His chest. Cold and wet.

Soaking us both.

"Jesus H. Christ." He sighs loudly enough for me to hear over the racket. The ruckus. "Let's get the fuck out of here."

A giant paw is at the small of my back, his mammoth body shielding mine as he shoves through the people standing in our way. Like a linebacker on the football field—or, a rugby player, I guess? Whatever position blocks people on the rugby field.

I've never seen it, so I have no clue.

The air outside is cold, or maybe it just feels like it because I'm drenched in alcohol, the yellow stain on my pretty dress running the entire length of the now sheer cotton.

The best part? I'm not wearing a bra.

Shit.

"I should text my friends to let them know I'm outside."

A curt nod. "You do what you gotta do."

Me: *Outside*

A few minutes slowly tick by before Mariah replies: *Outside where?*

Me: The party.

Mariah: I left.

What does she mean, she left? Without telling me?

Me: Where are you?

Mariah: I left like, an hour ago?

Me: Why didn't you tell me???

Mariah: You were busy filling beer cups and stuff.

Me: No, I wasn't. I've been waiting for you all night. I didn't even want to be here.

Mariah: Whatever. The point is, I'll be home in 20. Right now we're at some guy Lance's house and then I'm bringing him home.

Me: What am I supposed to do while you have some guy in our apartment?

Mariah and I share a room because we pay our own rent, live in a one-bedroom, and can't afford anything bigger. It sucks, but at least we have our own place and don't have to live in the traditional dorms—or one of those horrible off-campus rental houses infested with bats and outdated everything.

I grew up living like that; I'm not doing it anymore.

Mariah: It's not a big deal, Teddy—just stay out on the couch.

Me: *And listen to sex noises all night?*

Mariah: *I mean…don't you have those noise-canceling headphones?*

Mariah: *Shit, GTG. See you in like, half hour. K bye.*

There is no way I can spend the night at home if she has a guy there! No freaking way do I want to listen to them banging all night—Mariah is stupidly loud when she has sex, I don't think I could stand her bringing someone home tonight. She thinks being loud is a huge turn-on for guys, but really it sounds fake and porny, and I can't believe she'd bring someone home without discussing it with me first.

That's always been our rule: before bringing home guests, male or female, give the other roomie a heads-up first.

My brows furrow, dipping deep, creasing my forehead.

"What's wrong?"

"Nothing." I spit it out in the way girls do when they're pissed but don't want to admit it.

A snort. "Is it really nothing? Or are you doing that thing girls do where they say it's nothing when it's actually something, and deep down inside you're pissed off and want to explode?"

I can't help it—I laugh because he's right. It is something, and I am kind of pissed.

"My roommate left an hour ago, went to a guy's house, and didn't tell me." I give him the abbreviated version. He doesn't need to know there is going to be a dude in my room having sex with my roommate in less than an hour.

"Well let's get you home then."

I wave him off with a sigh. "I can't go home. She's bringing the guy back to our place."

He glances toward the rugby house, gives his beard a few strokes. "So?"

"She and I…share a bedroom."

"Well shit." His drawl drags out, and this time he does sound like a hillbilly. It sounds like he's saying *whale sheet.* "That ain't cool."

No, it's really not. Mariah knows I won't want to be in the apartment with a strange guy there. She knows this and yet she's doing it anyway instead of staying at his place. Or asking me first.

"It's fine. I'll sleep on the floor in the hall outside our apartment."

Fluorescent lights. A stiff couch thousands of people have sat on. Probably a student or two or fifty will see me sleeping there and think I'm a loser.

Awesome.

The guy's chuckle is deep, vibrating deep in his broad chest. He's thoroughly amused. "You're not sleeping in the GD hallway."

"The GD what?"

"God damn."

The amused look on his bushy face turns to unexpected irritation, making me laugh despite myself and the circumstances, one of my shoulders shrugging. Pulling at the wet dress plastered to my chest, sending a cool shiver down my spine.

I hug myself, rubbing at my upper arms. Shiver. "It's not like I've never done it before. It's only one night, and I can take a nap tomorrow."

"No. Fuck that." He runs a hand through his hair, fiddling with the rubber band holding it back. Yanks it out, pulling it loose and shaking out his hair.

It's a lion's mane, hitting just below his shoulders, wild and tangled and beautiful. A beautiful mess.

With two hands, he scoops it back up, twisting it into a knot, the black rubber band looping around the strands as he mumbles, "Your friends are assholes, I swear to fucking God. Why do you put up with their shit?"

I allow my mouth to fall open, because honestly? This night has gone to complete shit.

"Please don't start with that again. You don't know them—or me."

"I know enough. They've ditched you three weekends in a row. If those were my friends, I would have told them to fuck off by now."

"Just like that?"

"Yup." His nod is terse. "Just like that."

"I'm not *you*—I'm not a barbarian, I can't just…" I wave my hand in the air aimlessly, searching for words. "I can't."

He turns his broad back, starting toward the stairs leading down into the yard, long strides taking them one at a time. When he glances back at me, he says, "Are you coming with me or not?" I hesitate, one foot inching forward. "Yes or no?"

Seconds pass and I bite down on my bottom lip. Where is he going?

It's dark out, obviously, and the only thing in the yard

is him, some trash, and a few cars parked along the curb.

Still, I haven't gotten any creeper vibes from him; if anything, he's been strangely...protective? Considering we don't know each other whatsoever, it's strange that the way my friends have been treating me lately seems to annoy him to no end.

So weird.

So...intriguing.

I hustle down the steps after him, trying not to trip and kill myself once I hit the bottom, my shoe catching on the lip of the concrete slab anyway. Thankfully, I keep my balance.

Look up, watching as he cuts across the grass, hands reaching for the hem of his black T-shirt, pulling the fabric up and over his long torso, presenting me with his bare back.

His *toned*, ripped back.

Muscles defined, his lattisimus dorsi is...

Is...

Um.

I try not to stare even though he can't see me, afraid that when he does finally whip around, he'll find my eyes molesting his front side the way they're molesting his rhomboid and trapezius, and holy shit, I can't believe I know what these muscles are actually called.

I also can't believe how incredible his body is.

It flexes when he balls up his shirt, walking to a shiny, black, luxury SUV parked at the curb. Its headlights flash brightly when he hits the remote to unlock it, cab illuminating as his voice calls out, "Get in."

Wow he's bossy.

And yet, before I know it, I'm inside the lavish vehicle, buckling the seat belt over my soaking wet dress, eyes fixed straight ahead out the window, carefully avoiding the naked upper torso he's strapped in on the driver's side.

The engine roars to life, purring. "Where are we going?" I ask quickly.

A long stretch of silence follows as he hits his turn signal and eases into the street. "My place."

What? No!

"To do what exactly?"

"Sleep?"

"No! No, it's fine, really. Just take me to the dorms— I'm in the upperclassman apartments on McClintock."

"I have a really nice place. You can crash with me. I really don't give a shit."

"I-I can't do that. I thought maybe we were going for cheeseburgers or something." *God I'm an idiot.*

"Why?" His face is contorted. "All we're going to do is sleep."

In the dark, I raise my brows. *Yeah right*, they say.

I'm almost insulted by his belted-out laughter. His cackle.

I cross my arms over my chest defensively. "What's so funny?"

"You thinking I want to sleep with you."

"I do not think that!" We both know I'm lying.

Another laugh. "Yes you do." Pause. "Look, it's fine— I'm not going to assault you or take advantage of you, trust me. I have zero interest in women, so your virtue is safe with me."

"Oh," I mutter. Then, "Oo*ohhhhhh*!!!"

He gives me a sidelong glance and rolls his brown eyes, which are brightened by the street lights. "I'm not gay."

"Oh."

"Don't sound so disappointed."

Now it's my turn to laugh. "Well then don't announce it like that. Being gay isn't a big deal—I wouldn't care, and it wouldn't surprise me if you were."

"I *know* it's not a big deal—but I'm not," he grinds out through perfect teeth. "But I knew that was what you were thinking."

"Fine. That's totally what I was thinking."

His grunt comes out of the dark, blinker for a right-hand turn ticking against the sudden quietness of the cab.

"How could you tell?"

"By the way you went *Oohhh*!!!" He mimics a high-pitched female voice so well my mouth curves into an amused grin. "All relieved and shit, like you just solved the freaking Pythagorean theorem."

I shoot him an agitated look.

"It's a math theory…"

"I know what the Pythagorean theorem is, thanks."

You don't earn a scholarship for engineering without adding numbers and knowing some basic geometry.

I might hate math, but I'm good at it, even though I still occasionally use fingers to do addition. Who doesn't? I have zero shame, unless I'm sitting in front of my geometry professor. "Just so you know what you're dealing with here. Don't ever expect me to add my way out of a dangerous situation without a scientific calculator. We will both lose in a big way."

"Seriously? Math is so easy, I can do that shit in my head. And all the Pythagorean theorem does is state that the square of the hypotenuse is equal to the sum of the squares of the other two sides and—"

"I know all this, jockstrap." I hold a hand up. "Please just stop."

I've had a few beers and don't want to talk about classes right now, especially mathematics.

Quick, what's fourteen plus thirty-seven? Answer: I have no damn idea, *leave me alone.*

"Do you want to stop by your place real quick and grab a change of clothes?"

I do a quick calculation of the odds I'll run into Mariah and whoever it is she's bringing home, figure it'll be safe to dash in if I make it quick, and nod my head.

"Yes, please. I live in Dautry."

"Got it."

"Thanks."

It takes me less than five minutes to race down the hall to our place (we live on the first floor), grab a tank top, shorts, and underwear out of my dresser, and run back out to the waiting SUV.

It idles in the still of night, a lone figure looming inside the cab patiently, his profile hairy and bearded, the outline of his topknot silhouetted in the dark.

I hide a smile.

"Thanks," I repeat once I climb back in, and I get a chin tilt in return.

Respecting that he's not in the mood for chatter, we don't speak again until we're finally on the outskirts of campus and out of town, turning into a residential area, the kind with families and professors, not students and party houses.

At the end of a driveway, he pulls into the garage of a red brick Tudor that looks like it came out of the pages of storybook.

"Uhhhh…" I drag the word out because I just cannot help myself. "This is your house? Do you live with your parents?"

I tug at my hemline, dragging it down over my knees. *Shit, am I about to meet his mom? What is she going to think when she sees me?* I look like a waterlogged Labrador, and I can't imagine what my makeup looks like.

Perfect. Just perfect.

"No." He pulls the keys from the ignition and hits the button to shut garage door, closing us in. "I live here alone."

"You live here. Alone." In this house, which is a thousand times nicer than the one I grew up in.

He doesn't look at me, instead pushing on the driver's side door and hopping out. "Are you coming in, or are you gonna ask me thirty more questions?"

I roll my eyes and grab my purse. "That was only like, three questions." Hop out of the car. "Why are you being weird?"

But he's already opening a door, light streaming from a small room at the side of the garage.

It's a laundry room—*he has an actual laundry room!*—shoes lined up by the door, a few sets of shirts and pants neatly folded and stacked in tidy piles atop the washer.

I am so confused.

Bending to unzip the booties I'm wearing, I slide them off, placing them by the door. Next to his giant ones. Smoothing my hands down the front of my dress, cringing when I hit the wet spot, I gingerly follow him across the tile floor and into a well-lit kitchen.

Onto the polished hardwood floor.

The kitchen looks state-of-the-art and updated, almost like a showroom, and I rest my hands on the cold counter, clasping my fingers to give them something to do.

I am so out of my element. I wasn't raised in a place like this, let alone live in one at age twenty-one.

Who is this guy and where does he come from?

Not the backwoods of Arkansas, that's for damn sure.

I bite my tongue to stop the steady stream of questions in my brain from vomiting out of my mouth.

Why does he live here? Who pays for it? Is he selling drugs on the side to pay for all this? Is he a trust fund baby? Who owns this joint? Why doesn't he have roommates? Does he have a job?

"Want something to drink?" he wants to know, standing at the sink, running the tap. Filling a glass and lifting it to his lips.

"Uh, surrre."

His long arm reaches over, retrieving another glass from the cabinet made of rich wood. Fills it and slides it slowly across the center island.

I cradle it between my hands, thumbs stroking the cool, smooth glass. Fidgeting, unable to keep still.

This whole thing is so bizarre.

***

KIP

Me: On a scale of 1 to fucking terrible, how bad of an idea was it to bring a girl back to my place?

Ronnie: Depends on the girl

Me: Hey big sister, I'm shocked you're awake! What the hell are you doing up?

Ronnie: The text notification woke me up, asshole!

Me: Liar

Ronnie: You're right—your brother-in-law just got done doing nasty, unspeakable things to me. Oh, sorry, was that TMI?

Me: Jesus Christ Veronica, I didn't need to know you were just having sex

Ronnie: Who said anything about sex?

Me: ANYWAYYYYYYYYY—about this girl...

Ronnie: Right, well, if she's already at your place, not much you can do about it, yeah?

Me: Gee, thanks

Ronnie: It's true. Besides, if you brought her home, she must not be terrible—we all know what you're like

Me: What am I like?

Ronnie: A complete freak?? I mean, look at what you did to your beautiful face just so girls would leave you alone. Now you're bringing them home? You must be hard up

"Um…so, you live here alone?" The girl's sweet but incredulous voice carries through my kitchen, her finger sliding along the edge of the cold, hard granite countertop.

"Yeah." I can't look at her as I dump my keys and phone onto the built-in desk next to the double ovens where I store all my crap, the texts from my older sister, Veronica, already forgotten. Everything glistens and shines because the cleaning lady was here yesterday morning picking up my shit, washing my clothes, folding them, and dusting what little putzy stuff I have set out.

Not my choice—she was hired by my mother—and Christ, if anyone found out I had a cleaning lady, I'd never live it down.

"Where did you find this place? Jesus, it's so nice."

"The landlord takes great care of the place," I joke, because *I'm* the landlord—but she doesn't need to know that.

She scoffs. "Who the heck are you renting from? No one who owns anything around campus, that's for sure. None of those guys give a shit—those houses are complete dumps."

She's correct; most of the houses are total shitholes, which is why I don't rent. I own this place—well, my parents do, but that's always been their thing: buying whatever house my sister and I happen to be living in at the time so we don't have to deal with rent and landlords.

"Who do you rent from? It can't be DuRand—his places might be nice, but they're not *this* nice, and not in this neighborhood. What'd you do, rob a bank?"

"Yeah, it's not DuRand."

I feel her staring at my back—my bare back because I still haven't put a clean shirt on—the wheels in her brain turning.

"*You* don't own this place, do you?" She pauses, eyes getting a bit narrower. "It's not a crime if you do, stranger person, I'm just curious. I'm not judging you for having a nice place to live in."

Stranger person? Is she talking about me?

I finally turn to look at her. "Stranger person?"

She plucks a grape out of the bowl sitting on my sleek center island. "I have no idea what your name is."

"It's Sasquatch."

"Stop it." She snorts. "I'm not calling you that—it's the dumbest name ever. What's your *real* name?"

God, I hate when people ask that.

She rolls those pretty eyes at me. "Just tell me. Stop being a baby about it."

"Kip." I push the word out grudgingly, squeezing it through the thin line of my lips.

"What!"

"Yup."

"Kip?"

"*Yes*," I grind out, nostrils flaring.

"Stop it," she repeats, wide eyed. "You're making that up. That is not your name."

"If I was going to give you a fake name, trust me, that wouldn't be it."

"Wow. Kip. Not at all what I pictured. I've been calling you Paul Bunyan in my head, sometimes Roy—you know, super redneck names."

What the fuck? "I do not look like a redneck."

"Yes you do." She tinkles out a laugh.

"No I don't." *Do I?* "Paul Bunyan has black hair, and his hair and beard are short."

"How would *you* know?"

"Haven't you ever been to Paul Bunyan's? The restaurant? There's a giant picture of him on the sign out front. It's like two stories high." Duh.

One of her brown eyebrows rises. "Can't say that I have."

"He has short hair." Why the hell am I repeating myself? Defending myself?

Christ.

She's eyeing me up and down—she's done it a few times tonight, always covertly, thinking I don't notice.

I do.

"No man bun."

I jerk my head and tug at my hair. "Nope."

"Well then. Kip." Her pert little mouth pulls into a smirk. "How very preppy of you."

"Shut up."

"Come on, it's super *Vacationing on Nantucket*—admit it." She's thinking again. "What is it short for?"

"Are you ready for it? Because your next laugh is on me." I sigh, long and loud. Rip off the proverbial bandage and wince. "It's short for Kipling."

She's holding back a smile, biting down on her bottom

lip—so fucking cute—crossing her arms over her beer-soaked dress when my eyes roam down the front. Over her high, round breasts and slim waist.

"Kipling. That's a pretty fancy name, you know."

"I know."

"I wasn't sure that you did, Kipling."

"Stop."

"It's also the name of a poet, Kipling," she informs me, as if I didn't already fucking know. "Rudyard Kipling—yikes, that's a mouthful."

"Can you not keep using it in sentences?"

Her brows go up, animated. "But it's so, so good."

"It's really not though."

"If you were wearing a polo shirt and khakis right now, it would make so much more sense to me, and maybe I'd lay off, but you're not—you were in construction boots tonight, and you're wearing a torn up T-shirt." Her eyes roam across my chest. "And brown cargo shorts."

When she averts her gaze, I'm surprisingly disappointed.

"I'm comfortable."

"Oh, I have no doubt about that." She snickers, looking me up and down, pops another grape into her mouth and chews. Swallows. "You don't mind that I'm stealing these, do you?"

I gesture widely. "By all means…" In goes another one, and I lean a hip against the counter, studying her. "Since we're sharing, what's your name?"

"Teddy."

"Like—the bear?" I can't help goading.

Teddy lets out a soft, lilting laugh. "Yeah, I guess. It's short for Theodora, my grandmother's name."

Theodora.

Romantic and pretty—kind of like her.

She has on a dress tonight, this one a little more daring than last week's cheerfully prim yellow one. It's baby blue, the thin material now plastered to her skin, with one of those necklines that goes over the shoulders and ties around the neck. I don't know what it's fucking called— halter or some shit.

Whatever. It's blue and short, and has matching ribbons in the back tied into a delicate bow, making the entire outfit way too feminine had it not been for the brown boots. I noticed them before she took them off in the laundry room. They're cute.

Way too cute for the rugby house.

Way too cute to be soaked in cheap beer.

Goddammit.

I run a hand down my face—down my beard—to prevent myself from totally checking her out. Or looking too long and hard at her tits.

"You want to shower while you're here, Theodora?"

"Teddy," she corrects good-naturedly.

"Right, like I'm not going to latch onto that one." I laugh. "Nice try."

"For real, call me Teddy."

"Only if you never call me Kipling ever again. Kip I can handle, but Kipling? Fuck that. *No.* Or just call me

Sasquatch like everyone else does."

"I will not be calling you by that hideous nickname, no matter how much it suits you, but I'll call you Kip if you call me Teddy."

A groan escapes my throat. "Fine."

"Good." My eyes shoot to the crown of her head as she nods curtly. "Then we agree."

"Shake on it?" When I stick out my callused hand, she draws hers back.

Pushes an errant hair behind her ear, glancing down at her feet. "We're good."

She's not scared of me, is she? I shove my hands inside the pockets of my cargo shorts.

"Shower?"

"I...yeah. I want to say no, because this whole thing is just so awkward for me, but since I'm starting to stink like a distillery, I probably should."

"You already stank in the car." My lips twitch at her shocked expression.

Her nose wrinkles. "Gee, thanks."

"I'm just fucking with you."

"Okay, well..." She hoists her clean clothes in the air. "Lead the way, I guess."

I don't. Instead, I point toward the staircase and flick my finger in that general direction. "Up the stairs, first door on the right. Root around for towels—I think there are some in there."

There should be, because my mom and sister came one weekend and didn't leave until the place was stocked and spotless. I had everything I needed when I moved in, like the pampered son of a billionaire would.

God I hope Teddy doesn't get all weird on me after she spends the night.

I listen to her softly padding away, her bare feet climbing to the second story then the door to the guest bathroom clicking closed.

The sound of the lock being turned.

I grin at that—her caution—leaning back against the counter, scratching at my stomach. Rise to my full height and stretch. Make my own way up the stairs to the master bedroom, intent on washing the filth off myself.

Which I'm used to—I've never left a house party without being covered in something disgusting, just like I've never left the rugby field without being caked in mud, grass stains, and dirt.

The hot water sluices off my body, my mind wandering to the girl in the shower down the hallway. She's not overtly sexy in any way, but I've never had a girl in my house, so naturally my hand strays south of the border.

I don't purposely picture her curvy hips in my mind, or the shape of her breasts pressed against the pale, thin fabric of her cheaply made dress.

It just…happens.

It also just so happens that I haven't had sex in—Jesus, I don't even know how long. Since sophomore year, if I had to guestimate. The year I decided I didn't want to be fucked simply because of my face or my last name, the year I grew the beard and let my hair get long and developed a chip on my shoulder because of the fairer sex.

It's not their fault—it's mine for believing a few of

them actually gave a shit about me.

The boner grows between my legs when I stroke it slowly, water lubricating—wet and warm—my eyes sliding closed as my fingers grip the base of my shaft.

For a tall guy, it's average as far as cocks go, but it's thick and always ready for a pull.

An arm goes up against the tile wall, empty hand bracing my body as the other one strokes. Glides up and down, up and down.

I moan, picturing Teddy in my shower, naked skin, tits and ass. Wondering if her pussy is shaved, waxed, or natural. Picturing her nipples in my mind, the color of her areolas. Their size. Whether she gets off on having them sucked…

I moan.

Mouth falls open, obviously, because it feels fucking great pumping away at my own cock. Yeah, I feel like kind of a pervert, but it's not my fault I'm suddenly having fantasies about her—I'm a warm-blooded, hormone-filled male, and there is a naked female in my house that I cannot—and will not—ever fuck.

Plus, I'm horny.

A hand is one thing, a pussy another entirely, and I haven't banged one in so long. Too long.

I barely remember what it feels like to sink inside one, so there is no reason I should be hard over Teddy…*whatever her last name is.*

She's cute, but not gorgeous. Wholesome, like the girl next door. Studious. Hardworking, if I have her pegged right—probably here on a scholarship.

I know her type.

Cheap clothes. Cheap jewelry. No car.

Worried about what her friends think and too afraid to tell them to fuck off.

I'm surprised she doesn't have more of a backbone, honestly. Her type usually does—the ones who have to fend for themselves, have to make their way in the world without the help of their parents.

My head dips, bowing, shoulders hunched as I stroke my slippery dick, tongue darting out to run along my bottom lip. Teeth biting down.

Eyes still squeezed shut.

Teddy filling the void behind my lids.

My cock filling the void in my cupped hand.

It's not enough, and I stroke harder. Rough. The grunt from my throat is low, echoing off the tiles in my shower, and I refuse to say the name tripping off the tip of my tongue.

Don't say it.

Don't you dare fucking say it.

I don't—but it's close—and when I come, it's hotter than the water that washes it down the drain.

I don't know how long I stand under the shower spray before rinsing the rest of my body, but it's long enough that Teddy is dressed and downstairs, curled up on the living room sofa when I finish and find her.

Nothing has been turned on, not the television or radio, and she's not playing on her phone. There's just the light from the kitchen streaming into the room casting a glow. Knees drawn to her chest, Teddy has a blanket in her lap, pulled to her chin, shoulders bare except for the straps of what must be a white tank top.

"Hey." She looks up when I enter the room, snuggling deeper into the blanket.

"Hey." I plop down in a leather chair across from her, propping my feet up on the wooden coffee table. Spreading my legs, I lace my fingers behind my neck—a better position to observe her in.

She eyes me up in the dark, but not in a calculating way. It's more like she's trying to decide if I'm going to pounce on her or whatever—if she should get the fuck out of the room or stay put.

I want to laugh at her aversion to me, and at the same time, I want to push her buttons.

It's late and dark, and I'm fucking beat, but I can't just leave her sitting here, alone.

Today ended up being shit, and it looks like that's how it's going to end. I have a strange girl in my house—the house that is my sanctuary—and I pray to God she can't remember how to get here. The last thing I fucking need is her dropping by unexpectedly, expecting something...

Then I'd have to be a complete dick, which would make me feel like an asshole. And I hate when I have to be an asshole.

Actually, that's a lie—I fucking *love* it.

But looking at her? I'd hate to be an ass to Teddy. She looks so sweet, curled up on my couch, snuggling in my blankets and *Jesus H. Christ, what the fuck am I saying?*

"Tired?" she asks softly.

"Yeah."

"You should go to bed."

"You trying to get rid of me?"

"No." She laughs. "Besides, it's your house. *You* probably want to get rid of *me*. I'm the one invading your space."

That's true.

"Nah. It's cool." I glance toward the staircase—the dark cherry balustrade, polished to a shine along with the counters, cabinets, and whatever else Barb scrubs when she's here. It leads to the second level, to the two guest bedrooms. "Take whichever room you want. They're both on the same side of the hallway as the bathroom."

"Thank you." She pauses, and I can hear her thinking. "I'll be gone first thing in the morning, promise."

"Whatever, it's not a big deal." I cross my legs at the ankles. "I'll probably be gone anyway—I run every morning."

"Oh? What time?"

"I generally hit the pavement by six."

"Wow, even on the weekends?"

"Yeah. We usually have matches on the weekends, so gotta stay conditioned."

"Matches? For what?"

"Rugby."

"You're a player?"

The way she says player gives me pause, and I search for a hidden meaning on her expression. When I don't find one, I give my head a terse nod.

"Yup."

There's a short hesitation before, "Wait, is the rugby thing intramural, or is it an actual university-sanctioned sport?"

"It's a sport."

"So do you travel?"

"Yes."

"Like…where to?"

"Same places the football and baseball teams travel to, if they have rugby."

Teddy wrinkles her nose. "I don't know where those places are."

"You're not a sports fan?"

"Nope. I mean, it's fine, but I don't, like, go to football games or anything."

"Why?" You can bet your sweet little ass her jock-chasing friends do.

"I just don't."

"Not even with your friends?"

"No. Those sports passes are really expensive."

Hmm.

"Maybe you'd like rugby better than those other sports anyway."

"And why is that?"

"Those other sports? The guys are all a bunch of puss-ies."

This gets me a laugh, deep and throaty and sexy. Teddy covers her mouth with a hand, stifling a snort.

My brows shoot up. "Did you just snort?"

She groans, drops her hand. "Ugh, you heard that?"

"I mean, yes? It was an audible snort."

And it was so fucking adorable.

"I hate when I do that."

"So you're a snorter?"

"Could you not call it that?"

"Snorter? Do you have a better word for it?"

"Not giving it a word is a better word for it. And not bringing it up again would be fantastic."

"But it's kind of cute."

"Stop."

I oink like a pig.

"Oh my god."

I oink again.

"Kipling."

No she did *not* just call me that. "Hey, we had a deal about the names."

"Then stop oinking!"

"That was a *snort*." I'm tempted to do it again. "Not to be confused with a fart. Two opposites ends."

Teddy sits up, indignant, blanket falling away and revealing her crisp white tank top. The shadow of her nipples beneath, chest rising and falling. "I do not sound like a pig when I snort!"

My shoulders give a shrug. "Tomayto, tomahto."

"Shut up!" But she's giggling when she says it.

"Fine, I won't make fun of you anymore."

"Good, because I hate it."

"Why do you get made fun of?" I'm teasing, but the silence that follows is enough to answer my question, and my brows furrow. "Who makes fun of *you*?" Teddy is the sweetest fucking girl I've met at this school—I mean, I've only known her for all of three seconds, but I doubt she'd intentionally hurt anyone's feelings. "Let me guess—your roommate and those other *friends* of yours."

More silence. "No. It's not my other friends."

"So just your bitchy roommate."

"Could you not call her tha—look, she's not bitchy, okay? She's just…" A diminutive shrug of her delicate shoulders.

"Do not—do *not* tell me she's misunderstood."

"She is who she is, I guess."

"And what is that?" A cock-blocker.

Jock chaser?

Selfish?

"We've always been opposites. Friends don't have to match. Friendships aren't perfect—you should know that."

"No, but guys are different. We don't have feelings, and if one of my friends treated me like shit, he wouldn't be my friend anymore."

Teddy rolls her eyes so far back, they're likely to get stuck in the back of her head. "Mariah doesn't treat me like shit."

Mariah.

Even the name sounds like a *Mean Girl* name.

Mariah: almost rhymes with piranha.

"Doesn't treat you like shit, you say? This from the girl sitting in some strange guy's living room, miles from campus, on God knows what street in the middle of the night because you couldn't go home, because she is *banging* some dude in your one-bedroom room apartment and she doesn't give a shit that you're not home safe."

Damn. That came out sounding way harsh, didn't it?

Still, it's the fucking *truth.*

"I-I..." Teddy stutters, and for a brief moment, I feel terrible.

Meh, kind of.

Fine, not really. I don't know her, I don't know her roommate—but I do know she needs to buck up and grow a pair of balls.

"Face it, Teddy, you need lessons on how to be a bigger bitch."

"Are you insane? The last thing I want to do is become a bitch on purpose."

"A badass then."

"A badass?" Her brows are up in her hairline. "Even that's a stretch for me."

"Fine. You need to grow a backbone."

"I have one! It's just...I'd rather choose what battles I want to fight."

"And how many fights have you ever been in?"

"None?"

"Arguments?"

"Er..."

"How many times has your good buddy Mariah swept

in and 'stolen' a guy you're talking to?" I use air quotes, and Teddy flinches.

"I don't know."

"More than one but less than five?" Jesus, why do I keep pushing this?

She shrugs.

"More than five but less than ten?"

"Kip! Who cares? If a guy doesn't like me for me and lets a girl like Mariah swoop in and '*steal*' him, I don't want him anyway!" Her voice is raised and she uses air quotes too, imitating me before crossing her arms over her chest defensively.

"If he doesn't like you for *you*? Is that the kind of bullshit girls tell themselves when they get rejected?"

From across the room, I see her mouth fall open.

Oops. Was it something I said? It looks like I kicked her puppy.

"So that's a yes."

Her mouth sets into a thin line, lips pursed.

"Teddy, there are rules, you know, and your friend breaks almost all of them."

"What rules?"

"Girl code and shit. I don't know—you should know more about this than I do. How to be a wingman and not a cock-blocker, how to date an athlete—shit like that."

"Come on, now you're just making stuff up."

"Rule number two: care less about what people think and more about doing what makes you happy."

"That's not a rule—that's an inspirational quote. Also,

what was the first rule?"

"Don't be a pussy." I can tell she's barely containing her impatience and cock my head to one side. "Why are you being like this?"

Her answer is to laugh again. "Because you're kind of a weirdo."

I wonder if she'd call me a weirdo—*to my face*—if my face wasn't covered with enough hair to keep me warm through a blizzard on a mountaintop. What would she say if she knew I was so ridiculously good-looking beneath this beard that modeling agencies would be knocking on my door wanting to blast my picture through every major sports magazine?

But that's just my humble opinion.

"I'm serious, Teddy—you're not going to find a boyfriend if you keep doing the shit you're doing at house parties."

"Who said anything about me wanting a boyfriend?"

"So you don't want one?"

"I mean…" She falters so long I know what her answer is going to be. "*Yes*, but there's no rush."

"Well that's a good, because it's certainly going to take you fucking forever to find one at the rate you're going."

I can't tell in this light, but I swear she draws back. "Kip, that's a shitty thing to say."

"But true," I persist, trying to put what I'm about to say next delicately. Or not. "You're not going to get a boyfriend playing bartender at the keg every weekend or holding your friend's beer while she's upstairs fucking random dudes."

"That's not what she's doing!" Teddy gasps.

I smirk knowingly. "It's not?"

"No!"

How so very wrong sweet, young Teddy is. "How would you know? Did she tell you that?"

"*No.*"

"Peter Newton. Kyle Remington. Archer Eisenhower." I tick the names off on my fingers, satisfaction curving my mouth into a smile. "She might not have told *you,* but they told *me.*"

"What are those, the names of future presidents?" Teddy jokes naïvely.

"No, Theodora. Those are the dudes your roommate has fucked the past three weekends while you were downstairs being all nicey nicey." If I had a beer, this would be the time I'd take a sip of it for dramatic effect. I unclasp my fingers, uncross my legs, and lean back in the leather chair. Exhale, loud and pleased. *Ahhh.*

"*What?*"

"Peter Newton. Kyle—"

"I heard you just fine. I just… There is no way. Mariah isn't like that."

"Okay. Whatever you say."

"Is she?" The question comes out slowly. Unsure.

One nod. "Yup."

I don't need to flip on the light to know Teddy is blushing.

"I just can't imagine her having sex with a guy named Archer Eisenhower," she grumbles.

"In his defense, he's not bad to look at."

She shoots me the stink eye. "Why do you even care, Kip?"

"I *don't*." Which must be a goddamn lie, because here I am, pressing the issue. This little slumber party of ours is turning into a goddamn therapy session, and it's my own fucking fault for inviting her here in the first place.

I should have—could have—left her to sleep in the hallway of her building.

"When is the last time your buddy Mariah helped you out? Or told you about her sex life when she wasn't bringing a guy home? Or waited around the house so you could get ready?"

Most guys wouldn't notice Teddy wasn't wearing any makeup the first night she appeared at the rugby house, but I did. And I bet the five thousand dollars cash I have stashed upstairs in a shoe box she had no time to get ready herself, because they weren't willing to wait.

I'm one of *those* guys—freakishly observant.

"I can help you." God, what am I saying? Shut the fuck up, Carmichael, or I'll punch you in your own goddamn face.

Skepticism is etched all over her pretty face, but she sits up taller. "Help me how?"

"Well." I settle deep into the chair, get good and comfortable. "For starters, I notice you hang back a lot. You shouldn't be doing that—join the conversations, man."

"You notice I hang back a lot…" She has an odd look on her face now as she tilts her chin to the side, her sentence trailing off.

"Yeah. So like, instead of talking to the dudes walking up to the keg, you're way too shy. You should be making jokes and shit. Even lame ones are better than going full-on mute—and why are you even standing by the keg to begin with? What the fuck is that about, Teddy?"

"Uh, I don't know," she says miserably.

"Right. Step away from the freaking keg and join the damn party."

"All right." She looks so confused, but I'm not even close to being done. "How?"

I.

Am.

On.

A.

Roll.

"Do you need a goddamn puppeteer to help you figure out what to do with yourself? Someone to tell you what to say and do?"

"You're being dramatic. I'm not that bad."

"Yeah you are. You need a…" I search for the word. Snap my fingers in the silence. "Hairy godmother."

"A what?"

I'm a fucking genius is what I am. "Hairy godmother. Like a fairy godmother, but a guy."

Honest to God, I just made that shit up, right now, on the spot.

Clever asshole that I am.

"Are you *high* right now?" Teddy isn't speechless, but she's pretty damn close. "You sound drunk."

"Sober as you are. Okay, that's not true—I had three beers tonight, so maybe not completely dry, but close enough." I am six foot four, after all; it takes a lot of fucking alcohol to get me drunk—like, a *lot*. Plus, I never would have driven her anywhere had I been drunk. Never. "My point is, you need help—mine, specifically."

"I'm not sure I need *your* brand of help—no offense, Kip." God that name...makes me cringe every time she says it. Can't she call me Sasquatch like the rest of them? "No offense, but what do you know about relationships?"

Oh, now she wants to get sassy?

Fine.

"For your information, I've been in a few relationships."

"Is that so?"

"Yeah." With girls named Mitsy and Tiffany and Caroline. Waspy, pure-bred socialites pushed at me by my well-meaning but interfering family.

I throw up in my mouth a little.

"When?" Teddy is impatient.

"I mean, if you want to get technical, high school. And freshman year."

"Your freshman year of high school? Are you serious?"

"College too, smartass—and it might have only been a few relationships, but I learned a lot from them."

"Like what?"

Like the fact that I never want to be in another relationship. And girls named Mitsy might sound fun and cutesy in *theory*, but they're actually pint-sized tyrannical Nazis, drunk on the idea of spending days dating me, lounging at the country club my parents belong to.

I shudder at the memory of her bubblegum pink, coffin-shaped nails.

"Listen Teddy, with guys, you have to come out and say what you want. No gray area—guys don't get it. And don't fucking lie or beat around the bush."

Teddy rolls her eyes. "Give me a break. How is that going to help me at a party?"

"I'm giving you pearls of wisdom here—would you listen? So what if it doesn't help at your bartending job?"

"Shut up." She laughs, though reluctantly.

"What I can tell you is what guys want, so don't go to a party and start pouring their damn beer. Everyone will take advantage. Do you want to be known as the girl who hands out red cups?"

"No."

"Do you want to be the girl who pumps the beer tap all night?"

"No."

"Do you want to be the girl who stands in the corner talking to the social outcast?"

"The social outcast?"

"Yeah—me." How was that not obvious? Duh.

But Teddy's laugh is light and amused, which tells me she disagrees. "You're hardly a social outcast."

Maybe not, but only because everyone is afraid to piss me off. I might be an *okay* guy, but I look like the occasional street beggar more often than not, and that makes people uncomfortable.

Although, oddly enough, girls do hit on me often enough to confuse me.

I'm not going to argue those points with Teddy, though. She wouldn't get why I do the things I do.

So few people do, because no one knows my secrets.

"Next weekend when you come to the house, I'll give you some pointers."

"Oh jeez." Her blanket rustles. "Maybe I should just stay home."

"Give up, you mean?""No, I mean—maybe flirting isn't my strong suit, especially at a house party. I'm way out of my league and we both know it. I should stick to libraries and coffee shops."

"You're not out of your league though." Any one of those idiots would be lucky to hook up with a girl like Teddy—but that's not what she wants, is it? To hook up?

Nope. Teddy is a relationship kind of girl, and that's what makes her so damn different. Even I know she's long-term relationship material.

She a wifer.

"Teddy, you're kind of being a pussy about this whole thing."

"You *cannot* keep calling me that."

"Calling you what?" I know she's not going to say the word that flows so freely off my tongue.

"A…*you know.*" I swear, she lowers her voice as if just the thought of the word makes her squirmy and uncomfortable.

"I have no idea what I always call you." My eyes widen, lending an innocent air to my expression, which she's probably hard-pressed to see in the dim light.

"You're so full of shit, Kip."

"For real though, enlighten me. I call people all sorts of things. Shitface, doofus, fucker."

"The P word."

"The P word, the P word..." I scratch my beard. "*Pussy*? When else have I called you that?"

"Uh—the first night we met? Like, four times?"

Did I? Huh. "Really, four times? That sounds so unlike me."

Actually it isn't unlike me, because I really do love that word. What guy doesn't?

Pussy, *noun*: a wimp or someone who's a total chickenshit. Won't take risks, overthinks everything. Scared of their own shadow.

Pussy, *noun*: a cat. Furry kitty. Pet-able. Purrs when I stroke it—if I ever wanted to stroke a pussycat, which I don't.

Which brings me to...

Pussy, *noun*: female genitals. Vagina. A place I haven't sunk myself into in far too long, and now that I'm thinking about it, the dick in my pants gets stiff.

I'm uncomfortable in these thin, mesh gym shorts, which, in hindsight, were probably a bad idea—though it's not like I *planned* to get a woody after I already jerked off once tonight.

Get your damn head out of the gutter, Sasquatch—the last thing you need is sex on the brain.

And sex with Teddy? Out of the question, even though

I'd fuck her any day of the week if the circumstances were different.

But they're not, and I'm going to graduate and be out of here, and then I'll never see this place again because I'll be working in corporate America and probably miserable.

And clean shaven.

Yay me.

"My services are available if you want them. No pressure."

"What services. Are you a tutor now too?"

"No—the hairy godmother thing. Those parties are boring as fuck, and helping you would give me something to do."

"I…I'll think about it." She laughs, pulling her hair into a ponytail and securing it with the rubber band wrapped around her slender wrist. Glancing over her shoulder occasionally, worrying her bottom lip, eyes darting to the kitchen and up the stairs. Almost agitated.

Strange.

"Uh, are you *look*ing for something?"

She jerks her head away from the entry of the hallway, startled. "I'm sorry, I just keep expecting your parents to walk in. It's making me nervous."

"They aren't here."

"I know, you said that—I just think it's odd that you live here. Alone. In this gorgeous house. Alone. What are you, twenty-one?"

"Twenty-two."

"Still not normal."

No, it's not her normal, but it's mine—and it's pretty fucking hard to explain to people, which is the exact reason I never bring anyone here, guys or girls. It's just not worth the long, inevitable, drawn-out explanation. Plus, I don't owe it to anyone; it's my business, and I like keeping it that way.

"Is it making you uncomfortable being here alone with me? 'Cause I can go lock myself in the bedroom."

"Oddly enough, no—you don't make me uncomfortable."

"Why is that odd?'"

"Because…look at you. You're huge and hairy, and I don't even think I'd recognize you if you shaved all that"—she gestures in the general direction of my face—"off."

She sure as shit wouldn't recognize me, which is the reason I grew this beard and keep my hair long.

"Do you ever…?"

I need more prompting. "Do I ever what?"

"Shave."

Obviously. If I didn't, I'd look like a ZZ Top reject. "Yes, I shave. I shaved this morning." I run a hand down the length of my beard, satisfied with the wiry hair that took me two years to grow this long.

"No, I mean, like—off. Do you ever shave that *off?*"

"What's wrong with it?" I stroke it again for good measure.

"Nothing is *wrong* with it, Kip. I'm just asking if it's ever not there."

"No."

"Oh." Pause. "How come?"

"Because I like it?"

"Fair enough." Her lips purse. "It's just…you're a bit young for the Grizzly Adams look."

"Who the *fuck* is Grizzly Adams?"

"A mountain man who wrestles grizzlies…basically."

"*Any*way." I give my eyes a heavy roll to end the conversation, and she follows me up the stairs. I point to a closed door on my left. "Spare room here, bathroom there, but you already know this. Obviously no need to lock the door behind you."

"Doors got deadbolts?"

I feel myself grinning. "Nope."

"Well, I'm not worried. I'm less your type than you are mine, I think."

That's where she's wrong—I'm warming to Teddy in ways I shouldn't be. I'll be thinking about her long and *hard* after we're both locked in our bedrooms tonight.

"Not worried? You're such a damn liar."

"How can you tell?"

A scoff leaves my throat. "Because you keep looking for the nearest possible exit."

"So I shouldn't climb out a window because we're on the second story? Got a ladder I can prop against the house?"

"Jesus Christ, don't even joke about going out a window. Use the damn door if you're going to escape."

"But do you blame me? You're kind of…" She waves a hand around in front of my torso.

"Abnormally large and hairy? Yeah, yeah, I get that a lot."

"No, I was going to say it's probably not the smartest idea to be in a strange house, far from campus and my apartment, with a strange guy I just met, especially since we've both been drinking and I don't know anything about you."

That's where she's right. This is a terrible idea.

But here we are.

My lips twitch beneath my scruff. "Just try to get some sleep, Theodora."

Her soft laugh fades as the guest room door inches closed.

"You too, Kipling."

Brat.

***

My phone pings in the dark.

Ronnie: Are you still alive?

Me: Go to bed, Veronica.

Ronnie: Ahhh, good. So she hasn't murdered you. Yet.

Me: This girl is harmless.

Ronnie: What the hell possessed you to bring her home?

Me: Her friends are assholes and ditched her at the house.

Ronnie: So? Why do you even care?

Me: I have no fucking idea. But...

Ronnie: Don't leave me hanging—it's two in the morn-

ing here and if you're going to keep me up, make it good. Your niece will be up in three hours and I'm going to look like complete shit tomorrow.

Me: *I—Jesus, I can't believe I'm saying this.*

Ronnie: *Oh damn, this is going to be good, I can feel it.*

Me: *You can't say anything to Mom and Dad. Vault*

Ronnie: ***rolls eyes** Do I ever tell them anything???*

Me: *Yes, last year you told them about the public indecency citation.*

Ronnie: *That wasn't to get you in trouble! That was to shock them because I wanted to see the look on Mom's botoxed face! I JUST WANTED TO SEE IF HER FORE-HEAD WOULD CREASE WHEN SHE GOT MAD!*

Ronnie: *It didn't by the way. So. Hilarious.*

Me: *Goddammit Veronica…*

Ronnie: *Okay, okay, I'm listening. Go.*

Me: *This girl—her name is Teddy*

Ronnie: *That sounds soooo East Coast, pleated skirt, cardigan-y of her.*

Me: *Stop.*

Ronnie: ***zips lip***

Me: *She's been coming to the rugby house every week-end with these bitchy friends of hers, and they keep ditching her, and tonight she didn't have a place to sleep. Like, I wasn't going to let her sleep in the hallway of her apartment.*

Ronnie: *How uncharacteristically chivalrous of you.*

Me: *So I brought her home and we started talking, and*

the next thing I fucking knew, I was volunteering to help her out.

Ronnie*: Help her out with WHAT??? God, do I even want to know?*

Ronnie*: Yes, yes I do.*

Ronnie*: And for the record, I just sat up in bed and turned on the light, and now Stuart is awake and he wants to hear the end of this story too.*

Ronnie*: BTW, since I woke him up, I owe him a BJ. So he says thanks.*

Me*: Jesus Christ.*

Ronnie*: GET ON WITH THE STORY, MY GAWD KIPLING. What are you helping this Teddy person with?*

Me*: How to date. I told her I'd be her hairy godmother.*

Ronnie*: You're kidding me right?*

Me*: No*

[five minutes later]

Me*: Are you still there?*

Ronnie*: I'm sorry, hold on. Stuart and I are laughing so hard we have tears coming out of our eyes.*

Ronnie*: Hairy godmother? Oh my god, Kip, where do you come up with this shit? Mom would DIE.*

Me*: You said you weren't going to say anything!*

Ronnie*: I know, I know, but…*

Me*: I swear to God Veronica.*

Ronnie*: RELAX, bro—relax.*

Ronnie*: Hairy godmother—what the hell even is that?*

Me*: I told her I'd teach her to be more assertive. She's* *way too nice.*

Ronnie: Omg. Do you LIKE HER?

Me: Yeah, she's nice.

Ronnie: "Nice." No. I mean—do you LIKE her, like her?

Me: No. She's just a friend.

Ronnie: Kip, do you know how many great love stories start that way? "She's just a friend."

Ronnie: Yeah—a friend you want to bang.

Me: Don't start with me. I do not want to bang her.

Ronnie: *Yet.*

Me: She's just a friend. Barely even a friend.

Ronnie: Mark my words, Kipling: this isn't going to have the ending you think it will...

★ ★ ★

TEDDY

I can't sleep—no surprise—for several reasons:

1. It's a strange house I've never been in, full of noises I don't normally have to listen to while I'm trying to fall asleep.
2. It's massive and I'm slightly intimidated.
3. There's a huge dude down the hallway.
4. There's a lock on my door, but he and I are alone, so this was probably one of the worst decisions I've made this semester besides living with Mariah.

Mariah.

What am I going to do about her? Do I have to do anything? I know she loves me—and the way she behaves? I've said it a hundred times (because lately, I'm always defending her) that's just how she is, how she has always been, really. Since we were young, she's always been hypercompetitive, and not just with me—with everyone.

I've learned that I just…have to stay out of her way. Stand back, let her do her thing, whatever that "thing" happens to be at the time.

Sports. Extracurriculars.

Boys.

Deep down, Mariah is sweet and giving and kind. Not everyone knows her the way I do, especially guys, because she never acts like herself when she's around them.

No. When she's around guys, she tends to laugh too loud, talk too loud, wear too much makeup, and dumb herself down. I don't know why—I've never asked—but I've learned to accept it. If that's how she wants to behave, who am I to tell her what to say and how loud?

Not that it would matter since she hardly listens to me anyway.

I roll toward the window in the dark guest bedroom then when the street light hits my eyes in the wrong spot, roll away, toward the door.

Stare at it.

I locked it, right?

I'm tempted to throw back the covers, hop out, and double-check, but I know I'm just being paranoid.

Besides, Kip? Grouchy, rude, crass Kip? Oddly, I feel

like I can trust him.

Stupid, I know, but there you have it.

He brought me home because he was worried, not so he could assault me.

And, even with the beard and the hair and the huge body, I can tell it would still be easy for him to pick up women. Even with the beard and the hair and the huge body, he's still easy on the eyes.

My eyes, anyway.

I roll to my back, staring up at the ceiling, thinking about the guy a few doors down the hall.

What is he doing in a house like this? Who owns it? Why are all the rooms professionally decorated? Did his parents die and leave him tons of money? Is he spending it wisely or blowing it all on stupid crap—like that expensive SUV of his?

I wonder how they died. Was it in a fiery crash or something worse, like an illness or disease?

That has to be the explanation—his parents died. Nothing else makes sense.

God, that poor thing!

Alone in the world and alone in this big house! No wonder he doesn't want to talk about his parents; their loss must have been tragic.

You know what else I wonder? If he's lying in his giant bed, thinking about me too. I know it's a giant bed because I snuck a peek of his bedroom when I was walking to mine, the large four-poster placed strategically between two large windows in the center of the room.

No.

He's not thinking about me—no doubt he's already passed out.

A guy like that wouldn't give me a second thought.

A guy like that would have his pick of girls on campus, long hair and unruly beard or not—that shit is so trendy right now. As I flop to my side, I wonder if he realizes that. He seems to think it's incredibly off-putting, when in reality…

It's growing on me.

FIRST SATURDAY

"Since when was Hairy AF such a bad thing?"

TEDDY

"I lay awake all night agonizing over something, and I feel terrible about being so insensitive."

Kip's brows go up as he pours himself a cup of coffee and leans his back against the counter, legs crossed at the ankles.

His hair is a mess, worse than mine—sweaty and sticking to his forehead, piled in a man bun, he's added a sweat band for his early morning run.

"I couldn't stop thinking about your parents."

"Uh…*why*?" His voice cracks as it warms up, not having been used yet.

"I'm really sorry about what happened to them, Kip."

"What happened to them?"

"You *know*," I hedge, waiting for him to fill in the blanks.

Instead, his body leans forward, head tipping at an angle as he waits for me to finish my sentence.

"You *know*…" I try again. "How they…"

His head cocks. Brows go up as he sips from the white, porcelain coffee cup.

Slurps.

I try again. "It must not be easy living alone. Lonely, even."

Kip shrugs his massive shoulders. "Beats living with roommates—or with my family."

"Kip!" I gasp in horror. "You can't say things like that!" I'm one step from making the sign of the cross.

"It's the truth."

"That is so wrong on so many levels!" My voice is an outraged gasp.

"Why are you acting so strange?"

"You're the one being impervious!"

He presses two fingers to his temple. "First of all, don't use such big words so early in the morning. Second of all—what the fuck is going on right now?"

"It must have been hard on you when they *passed*."

"What are you talking about?"

"Your parents…*passing*."

"Wait—you think my parents are dead?"

"I mean, why else would you live in this house all by yourself?"

"Because they bought it?"

"Who did?"

"My parents?" He's staring at me like I've officially lost my mind.

"Wait, so—they're *not* dead? They haven't passed?"

"Stop saying passed—you sound deranged." He laughs. "No, they're not dead. The only thing my parents pass these days is the salt at the dinner table. Jesus Christ, Teddy, relax."

His voice cracks as he lets out a loud bark, bending at the waist, really milking this for all it's worth. *I feel like such an asshole.*

My eyes narrow into slits. "I hate you right now."

"What the hell did *I* do!" Kip can barely catch his breath. "I never said my freaking parents weren't alive, you just assumed they were. Oh my god, this is too good. It's too good."

"But…"

None of this makes any sense.

"Wow. You just made my day, I swear—goddamn you're cute."

"But…why would they buy you such a nice house? Why not a dump closer to campus? Who *does* that?"

When Kip presents me with his back, his shoulders give one last shake, hands busying themselves on the countertop by ripping open a packet of sugar and ignoring my question. "Let's not get into it."

Okay, so he doesn't want to talk about it.

Fine.

"Someday, though? If we're gonna be friends, Kip, we should be able to talk."

"Jesus," he mutters with a snort. "This is why I play rugby and stay away from girls."

"Why? Because you don't like having friends?"

"Yes." He turns to face me. "No, because girls make everything complicated."

Complicated?

"Are you being serious right now? I didn't say I wanted to marry you! I said I wanted to be friends. That wasn't a proposal—settle down, big guy."

God, why are guys like this? It reminds me of the time my friend Sarah invited this guy Dave to a baseball game; when she offered him one of her spare tickets, he said he couldn't go because he wasn't *ready for a relationship.*

Idiot.

We had a good laugh about it afterward, but the point is: sometimes guys are way more drama than girls are.

It seems like Kip might be one of those guys.

It takes everything I have not to keep rolling my eyes at the grown man-child standing in front of me, but I manage. He's being so ridiculous right now.

"Fine. You want to be my hairy godmother, be my hairy godmother." I sniff. "And if you don't want to be friends, we won't be friends. *Gotcha.* That we can do."

Kip tips his head back and talks at the ceiling. "Now you sound butt-hurt."

"Me? Butt-hurt? Please." *As if.* "I'm just clarifying."

There is no hiding that stupid smirk on his dumb face. "Don't worry—I get it."

I lean back in his kitchen chair and cross my arms. "What exactly is it you think you get?"

One of his giant paws waves in the air. "I get how girls

are. You want a relationship, I'm a good-looking, single guy, I have this house…"

"Oh my god—stop before you make me laugh."

"Whatever, Teddy. You know it's true."

"Are you insane? You sound crazy."

"You see all this"—he gestures those hands up and down his upper torso—"and I become a *prime* target."

I push myself up, rising from the table. "*You* are delusional."

He snickers. "Then why are you getting so defensive?"

Why is he so infuriating all of a sudden? "I would strangle you right now if I could reach your throat without a stepstool." As luck would have it, there aren't any to be found.

Kip laughs, and I'm sure his Adam's apple is bobbing somewhere in his stupid, bearded neck.

"You're telling me you don't want to date me? After seeing my house?"

"What part of *anything* I said this morning would make you leap to that conclusion?" I swear, guys are morons.

"When you said you wanted to be friends, you said *friends*—it was kind of hard to miss the inflection in your tone."

"Oh my god. I can't with you right now. I'm leaving." Everything I brought with me last night is folded neat as a pin in a tote bag, ready to go. "Thanks for the hospitality. It's been swell."

I throw him a two-finger peace sign for good measure, starting toward the door, pulling my jacket on along the way.

"Aren't you forgetting something?"

I don't bother turning toward him. "What," I clip out, agitated.

"You have no idea where you are."

"Pfft. I can map it on my phone." Duh.

"All right. Go ahead." He slurps from his mug, loudly and obnoxiously—on purpose, no doubt.

"I'll just do it now, if you don't mind, since it looks a tad chilly outside."

"A balmy forty-three degrees," he clarifies with a bright smile, whiskers covering most of his white teeth.

Forty-three degrees?

Lord, shoot me now.

I fiddle with my phone, typing in the address to my apartment and wait for our location to populate. Glance at the screen, then up at Kip, confused.

"Three miles! What the hell! Three miles? Seriously, why do you live so far away? Are you insane?"

"Some of us have cars," the bastard replies. One of his broad shoulders goes up then comes back down nonchalantly, mouth smug. "You still up for that walk? Or do you want me to drive you?"

"I hate you right now."

"That's the second time this morning you've said that—keep it up and I'll almost believe you." He sets the mug down on the white countertop. Brushes his hands off on his gray sweatpants and rises to his full height. "Let me grab a sweatshirt and we'll go."

Why am I powerless against this guy? He is so bizarre

and bossy.

And rude.

"Fine." If he insists on driving me home, I should shut my mouth and stop complaining about a warm, free ride.

When Kip is done gathering up a hoodie and pulling it down over his mass of messy hair, he grabs his keys and yanks the back door open. With a sweep of his hand, he ushers me through first—like a gentleman would do if one were here—and then we're out in the frigid cold.

"Thanks for the ride," I mutter when I'm buckling my seat belt. The least I can do is thank him for his hospitality.

"Don't sweat it. My sister would kill me if I let you walk home by yourself—last night or right now."

"Your sister?"

"Yeah, Veronica, but I call her Ronnie because she hates it. She's older and into manners and all that other bullshit."

"Ahh, I see. Did she raise you?"

"My parents are not dead, remember?" he deadpans, shooting me a raised eyebrow.

Oh shit, that's right. Why do I keep forgetting? It's pretty much the worst slip-up, ever. "My god, I am *so* sorry."

"You're going to give me a complex if you keep talking like that. I'm going to want to actually *call* my mother to hear the sound of her voice, and that will only confuse us both."

"Why? Don't you ever call home?"

"God no." He pauses, hitting the turn signal and heading toward campus. "No, that's not true. I guess I call enough—mostly texts and shit, though. My asshole sister's favorite thing to do is put us in group texts." Kip hangs another left, already knowing where I live and how to get there, and it feels like he's driven it a thousand times before. "Family group texts seriously want to make me gouge my eyes out."

"Why?"

"Dude, because. My mom never finishes her sentences. She will send three words, hit send, then type another two words and hit send. Then another two—hit send. To make one complete sentence, instead of typing the whole thing out, right? Then she'll send a GIF. Then four more words. Send. It makes me fucking *mental*. Ronnie knows I can't handle it."

That does sound horrific, but not unlike any of the group chats I've ever been in with my friends.

"My mom does the same thing. Kind of. But then again, there are only two of us, so I don't have to worry about an entire *family* chiming in."

"You're not missing out."

"I'm not?" Honestly, it sounds kind of nice.

"Fuck no!" Kip's SUV makes a right at the stop sign before he asks, "So, no brothers or sisters?"

"Nope. It's just me. The lonely only."

"And your mom."

"Yup, just me and my mom—always has been, since, you know…my dad left."

Most people ask what happened to my dad—or sperm donor, as I started calling him when I realized what a piece of shit he actually was—and I hope Kip isn't one to pry.

He is.

"You said your dad left, but what happened? Did he die?"

"No, nothing like that, although I'm sure my mom wishes that were the case. Haha."

"Hey, sue me for asking. You seem fixated on death for some reason, so I thought maybe that was why."

He has a very good point. "My birth father and mom were never married, and he took off when I was little; I don't remember him being around. After he left, we lived with my grandparents for a while."

"Ah, I see."

Yeah.

"So what's your mom do?"

"Like, what's her job?"

"Yeah."

"She…" I clear my throat and straighten my spine. "She's a bartender. And she waitresses."

I wait for the awkward pause that usually follows that statement, but it never comes. Don't get me wrong, it doesn't embarrass me that my mother is a bartender and waitress—it's *other* people who get all weird and judgmental about it.

Especially women her age, ones with husbands and families and minivans and carpools. That was never my mother, never us. We never had the money for that kind of life—barely had the money for me to play sports or join clubs.

Always just squeaking by.

I was left alone a lot. Not only did my mom work a lot when I was growing up, she couldn't afford babysitters or whatever. Taking every available extra hour, working overtime to pay the rent and utilities, at the same time saving for my college education.

"Damn, do you ever get to see her?"

"Sure I get to see her. I mean, not a ton…not really." If I'm being honest, my mom works way too much and I rarely get to spend time with her. "I, uh, I'm here on a partial scholarship, so…" The sentence trails off. "And I was just awarded a grant from the engineering department."

"Is that your major? Engineering?"

"Yes."

"What kind?"

"Civil." I pause. "Does that sound boring?"

"No—not at all." He reaches over and turns down the volume on his radio. "So you have a partial, and a grant, and your mom busts her ass to pay for the rest."

"Exactly."

"I get it."

"Do you?" Somehow I doubt it. I glance at Kip out of the corner of my eye, at the leather and chrome interior of his luxury vehicle, the branded logo on the sleeve of his pricey sweatshirt, not to mention his little slice of suburban heaven tucked away in a high-end neighborhood.

For a caveman, Sasquatch sure has expensive shit.

If he senses me eyeballing him, casing my surroundings, he chooses not to mention it.

"What's your major?" I ask out of polite curiosity.

"Economics."

"Wow. Really?" I'm sincerely surprised.

"Yeah. Business and economics seem to be in my future."

That's an odd way of putting it. "Why is that?"

"Family business."

"I see. Do you have a choice?"

"Kind of, but not really." A master of deflecting, Kip changes the subject as he slows down when we near the edge of campus.

"Have you ever lived in the dorms?" I cock a brow.

"Uh, no."

"Why not?"

Shrug. "My parents wanted me off campus."

That makes no sense. From my experience, most parents keep their kids on campus as long as they can—at least, that's what my mom wanted.

"Why?"

Instead of answering, he shrugs.

Kip measures his words. "It's complicated."

"Then I'm not going to ask."

"Thanks."

I catch a smile, a flash of his straight, white teeth. "You should smile more."

"I smile plenty." His face scrunches up, lip furled.

"You really don't though."

"Sure I do—you just have to catch it at the right moment. Sometimes you don't see it happening."

"Because of all the hair on your face?"

"Correct."

Despite myself, I take him in, his whiskers highlighted by the sunlight streaming into the driver's side window and through the windshield.

"Don't girls get whisker burn from your face?"

A short laugh. "No."

Pfft. "Yeah right."

"I'd have to kiss one for that to happen."

"You haven't kissed a girl?"

He rolls his eyes.

"Oh." *Ohhh*... "Now it all makes more sense."

"What does?"

"You being into guys."

He shoots me a quick glance, brows furrowed. "That's not what I meant and you know it."

Yeah, I know that wasn't what he meant, but it's fun to tease him. He's so serious.

My laugh fills the cab of his SUV. "You should see the look on your face—you look like a serial killer." One who's not amused.

"Ha ha."

"I would have said Bigfoot instead, but that seems too obvious."

"I *do* get that one a lot."

"Figured. That's why I went with serial killer, although you don't *really* look like one of those, either. You're too tall."

My stomach chooses that moment to growl, and it's so loud it fills the sudden silence.

Of course it does.

"You hungry?"

There is no denying it when my stomach rumbles again. "Uh, kind of."

"Why didn't you eat anything?"

"I wasn't about to go digging through your cabinets."

"Why?"

"Because I barely know you—it would have been rude."

"You want to stop somewhere and grab something?"

"No! No. It's okay, I have food at home."

"You sure? What about that little diner on the corner of South and Meridian—they make a killer omelet."

I mentally calculate the meager change stuffed inside my wallet. It's barely ten dollars and the only cash I have.

"Yes, I'm sure, but thank you for the offer."

"Come on," he urges. "Do you have somewhere else to be right now?"

"Don't you? You're the one with rugby practice today, right?"

"Later. At noon." His car is no longer headed toward my apartment, damn him. He's the shittiest listener; I'll have to remember that from now on.

"Kip, it's fine. *Really.*" I cannot spend my money on food when I need it for rent, books, and tuition. Frivolous spending is not in my budget for the month.

But for some reason, he isn't letting it go, and he isn't taking me home.

"My treat."

Well. In *that* case. "Fine—twist my arm." Because honestly, I'm starving, and food from an actual restaurant sounds like heaven. Cinnamon roll? Eggs? Breakfast sausages?

Yes, please.

***

KIP

Jesus, where is she putting all that food she ordered?

Seriously, Teddy is tiny—compared to me. I guess for a girl, she's pretty average, but next to my six foot four? She's pocket sized.

And she's stuffing breakfast links in her face with a forkful of egg and washing it down with chocolate milk. It's more than I'll pile in my mouth at once.

"Is that going to be enough food for you? Sure you don't want to order more?" I tease, eyeing her plate of eggs, hash browns, and the side order of a giant cinnamon roll. The quantity rivals mine, and with both our heads bent, we go at it, stuffing our faces like we haven't eaten in days.

I'll pay for this during practice by running it off with extra laps around the field, but right now, the greasy breakfast is worth it.

Even if I end up with the shits later.

I shovel a spoonful of food into my mouth and chew, wiping my mouth with the sleeve of my sweatshirt, totally cognizant of the fact that if my mother saw me right now, her mouth would fall open in horror at my complete lack of decorum, my complete disregard for the manners she drilled into me from day one.

"Gross, you have eggs in your beard." Teddy's lilting, soft voice floats across the table, half amused, half disgusted.

"Where?" I don't tell her that half the time when I eat, food ends up in my beard, a hazard of having so much hair hanging from my face. "Show me."

"I'm not touching it."

I snicker into my napkin as I swipe it across the lower half of my face, tempted to throw in a *That's what she said* but think better of it when her lip curls up and her eyes narrow like she knows I'm thinking it.

I don't even have to say it.

Nice.

"Don't say it."

I shrug. "I wasn't going to."

"But you were thinking about it."

I laugh and egg flies out of my mouth. Teddy's disdain grows, lip now completely curled up under her pert little nose.

"Yeah, I almost said it."

"Wipe your face, Kipling."

Ugh, that fucking name. "Dude, I can't help it if shit falls out of my mouth."

"You're disgusting. I'm never eating with you again."

"I have a feeling you'd eat with me every night of the week if I was paying for it."

Teddy considers this, finally nodding. "You're right, but only because my budget is so tight moths fly out of my wallet when I open it."

"That's sad." The words leave my mouth before I can stop them. Insensitive as they are, Teddy doesn't so much as blush.

"Poor me, I know. Feed me, Kip!" Her laugh is punctuated by the fork in her hand stabbing at the sausage on her plate, metal meeting porcelain, her moan fills the air between us as she stuffs the entire thing in her pretty mouth.

"Now who's the slob here? You don't have to be a pig about it because *I* had food in my beard."

She rolls her eyes pretty damn hard. "You're also *spitting* food out."

No shit, but, "Not on purpose."

She flops her fork in the air, pointing it in my direction and squinting. "Still, didn't your mother teach you any manners?"

If only she knew. Not only did my mother teach me manners, she hired etiquette coaches to come to the house and drill manners into Veronica and me—actual fucking etiquette coaches like it's the year 1845 or some shit.

No one can tell Lilith Carmichael what to do, and what she wanted was for her children to be impeccably mannered and well-behaved. And we were.

For a while.

Then, my sister and I became two teenagers who hated the watchful eyes of our parents, their staff, and the media. Our parents weren't just wealthy, they were celebrities in our corner of the country, Dad appearing on news broadcasts, buying up a professional football team when his net-worth topped nine figures.

Everyone knew our family, and Ronnie and I hated it.

The fact that I call my sister Ronnie? My mom hates that more.

"Are you listening to anything I say?"

"Huh?"

"You do that a lot you know—zone out." Teddy is back to picking at the food on her plate with the tines of her fork, pushing the scrambled eggs to one side, wry smile plastered to her face. "Sorry I'm so *boring*."

Shit.

"You're not boring."

"I kind of am."

"Would you stop?"

"Next you're going to tell me you have a lot on your mind."

"That's not what I was going to say because it's not even remotely true. There is nothing on my mind." I laugh, grabbing a hunk of toast, folding it in half, and stuff it in my gullet. I can't very well say *I zone out when you talk because I'm reminded of all the secrets I don't want anyone finding out, and you just discovered the second biggest one I have.*

The first being my family's ridiculous wealth.

The other is my giant, fancy fucking house off campus with its Egyptian cotton sheets and granite countertops no twenty-two-year-old on the planet should already own, because *what the actual fuck.*

Thanks Mom and Dad for making it impossible to have a normal life, or a relationship with a girl who doesn't care about that shit.

Whatever. I'm over it.

Still. My nostrils flare as I rip the paper napkin in two, balling up the pieces and tossing them to the far end of the table.

"So," I clip out. "When a guy comes up to you and says he likes your shirt, what do you say?"

A well-manicured brow shoots up into Teddy's hairline. "No guy is going to tell me he likes my shirt. My boobs, maybe."

"Your dress?"

Teddy heaves a sigh. "Kip, do we have to do this right now? I'm trying to eat my free breakfast."

"My coach always says practice makes perfect, Ted."

"Please don't call me that."

"Why? It's an awesome nickname."

"Because Mariah calls me Farmer Ted and I hate it."

"Mariah calls you Farmer Ted to be an *ass*hole and to put you in your place. *I'm* calling you Ted because I think it's adorable."

"It's a *man's* name."

"So is Teddy."

"No it's not."

So argumentative, this one. "Uh, Teddy Roosevelt?"

"Fine." She sighs again. "It's a man's name, but don't call me Ted."

"Fine." My hand moves across the table, toward her plate. "Are you going to eat that?" Fingers grapple for her toast.

She slaps my hand away. "I will stab you with this fork if you touch my carbs."

Shit. Hangry Teddy is savage. "What about the sausage?"

"I came here specifically for the sausage."

"Here for the sausage," I repeat, leaning back in the plastic booth seat, not even trying to conceal my snicker. "Good one."

Never has there been a bigger eye-roll from someone so tiny. "Shut *up*, you moron."

Teddy spears one of the brown links of meat, jiggling it in my direction. It wobbles on the end of her fork, up and down between us.

"Is that an offer?"

"You can't have it—I'm just torturing you because I know you're still hungry. You only ate one plate of food, you lightweight."

"Whatever. I can just get another side order if you're going to be greedy with your meat," I whine.

"You would have already ordered more meat if you wanted it. Admit it—you just want to take this because it's mine, and you're a spoiled brat."

"But food tastes so much better when it doesn't belong to you. Just like so many other things that aren't yours taste good."

Christ, that came out sounding so perverted...or maybe it didn't and I'm just a pervert?

Other things taste good, like...

Dessert. Sweets.

Pussy.

Pussy? Where the hell did that come from? Jesus Christ, Kipling, you're in the middle of eating breakfast.

But, now that it's on my mind…

My eyes travel south. Even though I can't see under the table to Theodora's lap, I imagine what her pussy looks like. Bet she keeps it nice and tidy too. Bare? Nah, she doesn't seem like the type to wax—plus, she can't afford it. Doubt she shaves it either, but I imagine she trims.

When I glance back up, Teddy is slowly shaking her head at me, emitting a little *tsk, tsk* sound.

"What?"

"I can totally read your mind."

Somehow, I doubt that.

"Trust me, no you cannot."

"Pfft, please—you might think I'm naïve, but I'm not." She mirrors my pose, leaning back in the booth, right arm draped over the back. "I know you're sitting there thinking about eating my breakfast. But you can't have it."

"Eating your…" The sentence trails off because I choke on the last word.

Breakfast—is that what we're calling it now?

Breakfast is not the only thing I'm thinking about eating right now.

Because I'm immature as fuck, a pervy asshole who didn't realize until *now* how perverted he actually was.

Now I do.

And it's because of *her.*

Shit.

"I'm not thinking about eating your food. It's safe."

"Mm hmm." She slowly takes a bite off the tip of a sausage link. Chews, a smile playing at her lips. "If you say so."

Takes another bite, then another, and I watch until the whole thing is gone.

"I *do* say so." Clear my throat and get down to business.

FIRST SATURDAY PART 2

"Guys are just gross."

TEDDY

"**N**ow." Kip's voice is low and croaks a little as he tries to get serious. "What were we talking about before? Oh yeah—you were about to tell me what you would say if some dude came up to you at a party and said he liked your shirt."

"We weren't talking about that, and we're not going to. It's stupid." I place another bite of eggs in my mouth and set about ignoring him. *Mmm, delicious.*

"Why aren't you taking this seriously?"

"Why do you *care*?"

"Honestly? I'm probably a little bored—give me something to do, would ya?"

Oh god. "The last thing I want to be is your pet project. It would be bad enough if you were female—I cannot handle having a random guy give me dating advice."

"First off, I'm not random—you just spent the night at my house. Secondly, you see the rationale behind that argument sucks balls, right? Taking advice about *guys* from a *girl*? Makes no fucking sense. I'm a guy—take advice straight from the source. I'm giving you a gift here."

"But you're not into girls."

Kip laughs. "Not right now, but someday I'm sure I will be…maybe."

"You need therapy."

"Actually, I've had tons of it. When I dropped out of Notre Dame to come to Iowa, my mother had a coronary and thought I'd gone off the deep end. Boom, therapy."

Boom, therapy?

He says the line so casually—*"When I dropped out of Notre Dame"*—like he was asking me to pass the salt.

"You got into Notre Dame?"

He scrunches up his face the way I do when I eat something sour. "Do you have to say it like that?"

He's avoiding my gaze now, the fingers of his left hand pushing and pulling on the handle of the white, ceramic coffee cup, tapping on it a few times with his fingernail.

"Yeah I have to say it like that." I'll admit, my tone does sound kind of *duh*, which is rude—but still. Notre Dame? You don't drop a bomb like that, leave it to detonate, and walk away without explaining yourself.

His grades in high school must have been insane. I couldn't have dared to dream of going to a school as illustrious as that, even if I'd gotten a full-ride scholarship with housing. No way.

And he dropped out.

Then I start to wonder…

"Were you there on scholarship?"

His eyes stay trained on the table. "No."

Well shit.

Non-scholarship kids aren't in my wheelhouse. I can't relate, nor do I have any friends who aren't receiving some kind of aid. So, having Kip sitting across from me with *all that money* has all the pieces falling into place.

The house.

The car.

The ivy-covered education.

His parents must be *loaded.*

I try not to let thoughts of *all that money* change my facial expression—try to keep the thunderstorm of questions at bay—but damn, it's difficult. A true test of my self-control because, despite myself, I am a nosy little bugger. My mom always said so.

Swallowing a bite of bread, I ask, "Are you glad you transferred?"

"Exceedingly."

"Okay Mr. Ivy League, calm down—no need to throw out the fancy words," I tease.

"Oh, I see how it's gonna be now."

"I mean, if I can't tease you, what fun would that be?"

"Fun for you, not for me. And keep that shit quiet, okay?"

"I will. You can trust me." If there's one thing I understand, it's not wanting the state of my finances—or lack thereof—spread around.

He's silent for a few heartbeats, staring intently into my eyes, heavy eyebrows still in a straight, serious line—

same as his mouth.

"Okay. I'll trust you."

My lips creep into a leisurely curve. "Good."

"You can trust me too, you know."

"Sure." More bread gets pushed between my lips and I chew then swallow it down with a gulp of juice.

"I don't have any friends so I don't repeat shit."

"You have friends. Don't be so dramatic."

"I have teammates—there is a huge difference. I don't tell those guys shit."

I consider this. "I used to tell Mariah everything, but… she's…"

"A loudmouth?"

"Yes."

"Would never have guessed that about her." Sarcastic ass.

"Shut up."

"Okay." Kip clamps his lips together, the hair around his upper and lower lips concealing his mouth.

"You are so hairy."

"Thanks!"

I laugh. "I bet when you shave all that off you'll look twelve. Right now you look forty-five."

"I'm never shaving this off, so…"

"Does your dad have a beard?"

"God no!" Kip laughs. "Oh my god, no—I can't even imagine my dad with facial hair. He's so buttoned up and stuffy he wears cuff links to brunch on Sundays. Plus, my mother—there's no way she'd let him."

Brunch on Sundays? Well *la-di-da*!

"Does the beard drive them nuts?"

"Yup, and that's the beauty of it."

"Ahh, now it's all making sense."

"What is?"

"You rebel. You're purposely doing all that to piss off your parents, aren't you?"

"No I'm not."

"Do you know how I can tell you're lying? You can't even look at me when you deny it."

"Whatever, Teddy. Can we stick to the subject at hand here?"

"You really must be bored. Fine, let's say I entertain the idea of letting you help me—you can't boss me around. That would drive me nuts."

"I won't."

I was right; he can't look me in the eye right now. "You're such a damn liar!"

"Tell me how I'm supposed to help without bossing you around! Go ahead, tell me." I open my mouth to respond, but Kip silences me with, "I can't. It would be impossible."

"Just don't be a jerk and we'll get along just fine."

"So you agree to let me help you?"

Do I? "Not really—it's more like you're wearing me down, like a dull pencil after too much use."

"Mission accomplished then, eh?" He looks oddly satisfied with himself.

I'm this close to planting a facer on the tabletop. "I can't believe I'm considering this—with you."

"You've been waiting for a guy like me to come along and help you."

"Stop making this my idea—it was yours. I'm still not convinced I should let a matchmaking giant follow me around."

"Hairy godmother—not the same as a matchmaker."

"Whatever. You're still being ridiculous, whatever you want to call yourself."

"You know, come to think of it, a hairy godmother would make an amazing Halloween costume. I'll have to remember that come next October." Kip stares off into the distance, imagining what it would look like. "Dude, like the Tooth Fairy, with tiny wings and shit? I could pull off a tutu, right? Camo would be badass—or brown."

A brown tutu?

"It would be pretty awesome," I relent begrudgingly.

"Hairy godmother, at your cervix," he jokes.

"If you went anywhere *near* cervixes," I mumble under my breath with a chuckle.

"Ha ha." He isn't laughing.

"*I* thought it was funny."

"Think we should establish some ground rules?"

"Probably—I can see you're getting overzealous and amped up to do this. If we could curb that from the beginning that would be outstanding."

"Me? Overzealous?"

And I'm becoming powerless to stop him. Or maybe curious enough to go through with it. He's crazy and fun—and perhaps I could use a bit of both in my life right now.

"Yes, you—you're like a bored frat boy, minus the frat, minus the boy, itching for something to entertain himself with. I am *not* that something."

"I hear a 'but' coming."

"*But*, I'm curious enough to go along with this stupid plan of yours." I mean, who could say no to that furry face? He looks like a dog. Or a shaggy lion. Kind of scary, but adorable.

"First rule: we are a team, Teddy, and there is no I in team. Write that down." He looks at me expectantly, but I don't have a pen. "Got a sheet of paper?"

I quirk my head to the side—I don't have that either. "Uh, *no*."

"Napkin it is then." Kip's brawny arm reaches across the table, fingers plucking a couple napkins from the shiny, silver dispenser. He whips a pen out of his man bun, and why he even has one in there is beyond me.

I waste no time. "Rule number two: the five-foot rule."

His pen hovers. "Five-foot wh…what is this nonsense?"

"I don't need you breathing down my neck. Five feet is close enough for you to stand while we're in public."

"How can I instruct you from that far away? It'll look strange with me stage-whispering from five feet away."

Oh brother. "I'm sure you'll get your point across in other ways."

"How will you hear me giving you directions?" The

level to which he is apparently affronted knows no bounds.

"Well, good point: I don't *want* you stage-whispering at me, let alone giving me *directions*."

"Then *what* is the *point*?" He taps on the table. "Two feet."

Oh, little guy wants to negotiate? Fine by me. "Four."

"*Three*."

God this is exhausting.

I nod, accepting three feet. "Next rule."

"Rule number three: you can't go home with anyone."

That makes me laugh. "*That* won't be a problem."

"It sure could be—guys will screw anything with a pulse. Someone will want to take you home if you're going to quit playing barmaid."

"Gee, thanks."

Kip shrugs, clicking his pen. "Rule number four: wardrobe."

He's going to nitpick my clothes? No. "You're not telling me what to wear. Look at you!"

His brown eyes roll. "This isn't about me. You're the one who needs help."

"Jerk! I do not! My clothes are fine—I didn't sign up for a makeover. God you're an asshole."

"*Fine* isn't going to have anyone hitting on you."

"You literally *just* said guys will screw anything with a pulse."

"That's true, I did say that, but we're looking for quality, not quantity."

He. Is. Infuriating. "Besides, I don't want those guys anyway."

"Good, because they won't be interested if that's the shit you're going to wear out." He smiles, laughing into his cup of coffee, barely concealing his idiotic smirk.

"Dickhead, this isn't about my clothes."

"It kind of is, just a lil' bit." He holds up two fingers close together. "We'll see. I'll put a TBD next to rule number four."

"Or don't, because we're done talking about it." Which leads me to, "Rule five: I get to veto any of your rules at any time."

"Same."

My eyes narrow. "If we're both able to veto rules then what's the point of having rules?"

"If you're the only one who can veto rules, what's the point of me helping you? You're not the freaking president."

"Oh my god."

He ignores me and drones on. "So, rule number six— I'm thinking can be something about you having to trust me, because I'm a guy, and I know what I'm talking about because I know what guys are thinking since I am one."

Wow.

Kips mouth opens again, but I interrupt what he's about to say next. "When it comes to guys, sure, but not when it comes to girls. You're about as subtle as a steamroller through a china shop."

"If we're being honest here, it's true that my size does me no favors."

"Aww, you poor, poor thing."

"Sarcasm does not become you, Teddy Johnson." Kip narrows his eyes and stabs his pen in my direction. "Rule number seven," he rolls on. "PDA."

Oh lord. And when the hell did he find out my last name? Was he searching for me on social media?

I roll the thought of Kip Carmichael creeping on me and secretly smile, the idea warming my insides.

"What about it?"

"Guys love competition. If someone thinks I'm interested in you, they are more likely to be interested in you."

That's the dumbest thing I've ever heard. "That's stupid."

"But also: true."

"So what's your point?" I shovel cold eggs into my mouth, chewing as he explains.

"If I have to put my arm around you, you can't punch me in the gut. You have to let it dangle there."

This raises a brow. "This dangling arm of yours—where is the hand at the end of it going?"

He pauses to stare at me. "Not on your *boob*. Chill out."

"Sorry, but the way you said it was creepy. Dangling arm over my shoulder? Gross."

"So?" He's impatient to write this one down. "Rule seven, you good with it? No punching me in the gut?"

"I'm so short, it's not your gut I'd be worried about if I were you." Then I tack a "ha ha" onto the end of the sentence for good measure.

"Teddy, be serious."

"Am I good with PDA from you? Suuure, why the hell not?" I mean, how often is he actually going to touch me? Probably never. Still, my eyes stray to his hands, his big man paws. They're large, a dusting of light hair on his knuckles, callused fingers gripping a blue pen, scribbling words across the napkin.

"Great." When he writes *PDA acceptable, no touching her tits,* I bite my tongue.

"No kissing," I add.

"Kissing?" Kip's head shoots up, and he sounds positively horrified. "Why would I *kiss* you?"

He sounds *so* horrified, in fact, that I start stumbling over my words. "I-I only said that because k-kissing is PDA. I didn't mean anything by it."

"Oh."

The silence that follows is painful. Clanging pots and pans from the diner's kitchen, the waitress taking orders, and talking patrons are the only sounds that meet my ears.

"I don't want you kissing me, Kip, *jeez!*" My eyes go to his hairy upper lip.

Ugh, as if.

His lips part. "Trust me, Teddy, kissing you isn't part of the equation here. My mouth won't be going anywhere near your face, so you can calm down."

I have no idea if that was an insult or not.

"I get that you're not interested, but you don't have to *say* it like that." My faces flushes as this conversation goes from bad to worse. "Forget I said anything."

Kip grunts, nodding. "Rule eight."

"You want to keep going?" Really? Because I no longer have any wind in my sails.

"Yeah, let's get these knocked out so we don't have to worry about it before next weekend."

FOURTH FRIDAY

"The night we learn Sasquatch has no patience for morons. Which is everyone."

KIP

"That guy is going to be your boyfriend—just follow my rules."

"Which rules? The rules we made up to keep you in line or the ones you're about to pull out of your ass?"

She has no faith in me, none whatsoever. "The ones I'm about to pull out of my ass."

Teddy crosses her arms over a perfect set of tits, and they push up into the low neckline of her black, off-the-shoulder top. It's tight, tucked into a pair of jeans, a simple pair of black boots skimming her kneecaps.

Understated and sexy, not that anyone here will notice.

Don't get me wrong, she looks pretty tonight, but she's still a tad too unassuming, with that *I require dinner, a drink, and long-term commitment before I'll let you fuck me* vibe, despite her efforts to the contrary—despite her obvious attempt to look sexy.

"At least you're honest."

"It's my only virtue," I admit, setting down the red cup I was handed on my way into the house tonight.

If I'm going to be playing matchmaker—correction: if I'm going to be her hairy godmother—I'll need to face this whole thing sober.

If you thought the idiots who lived and partied here were annoying *sober*, imagine how annoying they are when they're drunk.

Though they'd be easier to tolerate if I got piss-ass drunk along with them.

Half the time, I want to plant my fist right into the faces of a majority of these dickless morons, so I need all the sobriety and inhibition I can manage.

I can't believe I'm trying to set Teddy up with one of these douchebags; it's such a shitty thing for me to do, knowing what I know about them. Take Ben Salter, for ex-ample—the creep is almost flunking half his classes, only able to maintain his enrollment status by sleeping with any and every TA who will fuck him.

Male or female.

And Derek Lawson? Last year he was on meds for the various STDs he claims originated from public toilet seats. Right. *Sure.*

Another two are spoiled, pompous, trust fund babies.

Granted, *technically*, I'm one too, but I don't go pa-rading my parents' money around, flaunting it like a little asshole. My parents might be loaded, but I'm not a com-pletely classless fuck.

Only some of the time.

"What do you think of my outfit?" Teddy asks from

below.

"It's good."

"Just good? I had to borrow this shirt and these boots from my friend Tessa—I don't have anything that shows skin."

"Yeah, it'll do."

"Wow, okay—thanks for the vote of confidence. I thought I looked nice."

"You do. Relax."

"What the hell, Kip? You know I'm not good at this, and you said you'd tell me if my outfit was shitty."

"It's not shitty—you look cute."

Her hands are on her hips now as she faces me, red-faced and disgruntled, the lines between her brows deep. "Whatever. Can we just get this over with so I can go home?"

"Don't be a quitter, Teddy."

"You know what? I put in a lot of effort tonight and you… That hurt my feelings."

"What did?"

"God, why are you so clueless?" She throws her arms up, defeated. "When I asked how I looked, you said 'It'll do.' That was so freaking mean."

"Hey, don't get upset. I can barely see you down there, shorty. Is that a dress or a shirt? I can't see the bottom."

"Shut up." She relents, giving in to a laugh.

"Seriously, Teddy—you do look really cute. Don't listen to me. I'm an asshole, remember?"

"Yes, you are."

"You're not supposed to agree with me."

"Agreeing with you isn't one of the rules."

"Rule Eleventy…"

***

TEDDY

"You're hovering." He has been on my ass since I got here, grunting and snorting throughout every conversation I've tried to have.

"No I'm not."

"Oh my god, Kip, yes you are. Who is going to talk to me when you're shadowing me like a lurker—it's weird. We said three feet, but could you please go away!"

He hasn't left my side all night, and he's definitely come closer than the mandated agreed upon footage. I can literally feel the heat from his body on my back.

"You don't have to get all pissy about it. I'm trying to help."

"How is tailing me going to help? You're scaring people away—and not just the girls. No one wants to talk to me."

"Shut up, I am not scaring anyone away—Tyler Wheatly had no problem coming over."

I huff, crossing my arms. "To talk to you. You're huge—no one even notices I'm down here."

"*I* notice you're down there."

"Yeah, yeah, yeah, you don't count."

I catch his long sigh. "I can see down your shirt, you know. Of course I'm going to trail you all over the room.

It's not a bad view."

He can see down my *shirt*? "Why didn't you tell me that sooner?"

"Teddy, I can see down *every*one's shirt—it's not like your tits are the only show in town tonight."

"I don't know how to reply to that." I glance down at my chest, at the lackluster cleavage peeking up above my modest neckline. "I barely have any skin showing."

"Bullshit. If those were popping out any farther I'd see nipple."

The nerve of this guy! "You told me to wear something that would show off my boobs! I even put on a push-up bra, and trust me, the straps are digging into my skin. I should find the bathroom and take it off."

That does the trick, and he backpedals. "I changed my mind. A guy should want you for your brains, not your tits. Pull up the shoulders on your shirt."

"What the hell is wrong with you?" My palm goes up and I pop it in his direction to shush him. "Know what? I can't deal with you right now."

"Well you're going to have to, because we have an ironclad agreement."

"Agreements are meant to be broken."

"Iron. Clad."

"Ours was made over eggs and sausage—I was hungry and tired. That has to count for something—duress, maybe?"

Arguing with him is worse than trying to have a serious discussion with a drunk frat boy—out of hand and impossible.

I poke him in the bicep to get his attention. "Did you have to be such a jerk to Mariah before?"

"Yes." Nonchalant and unapologetic, Kip leans against the wall. "She deserved it."

When I arrived with my roommate not too long ago and we found Kip waiting for me on the far side of the room, Mariah wasted no time leaning into him, crooking her finger so he had to lean down to hear what she had to say. I watched, dismayed as her lips grazed the shell of his ear, followed by her tongue. Watched as his glower deepened with every word she spoke until he straightened up and told her she was a shitty human.

To her face.

"She was hitting on me."

"No she wasn't. She was just flirting." In her special way. "She's always like that."

I mean, maybe she *was* hitting on him. I have no way of knowing; Kip refuses to tell me what she whispered in his ear...before licking it.

"She was hitting on me, Teddy. Not flirting."

I poke him. "What did she say to you?"

"Trust me, you don't want to know."

He's right. I don't.

But I kind of do?

"Maybe you misunderstood her?" God, what am I saying? Even I know whatever she said to him, there was probably no way for him to misinterpret.

"Teddy, she was hitting on me, knowing you were here to meet me. She licked my fucking ear and bit the lobe—that is fucked up."

She bit his ear lobe?

I blanch.

He's right; she did know I was coming to hang out with him and she did it anyway. Licked him. Bit him.

A little knot loops itself around my stomach and tightens. Squeezes into a dull ache that moves to my chest.

Kip's truth hurts.

"But she knows it's not like that with us."

He studies me, stroking his beard. "Did you tell her that?"

No.

I don't have to say it out loud—he can see it written on my face, and he smirks, one corner of his lips tipping up...I think? His beard is covering his mouth, only the bottom lip jutting out in an irritated fashion. Briefly, I can't help but wonder what his top lip looks like, if he has an arched bow, if the rest of his mouth is full or thin.

I give him a once-over, starting at his booted feet, moving up his long stretch of leg. Glancing over his red shirt and unzipped blue sweatshirt. The tan skin. The hair.

He's kind of...

A sight to behold.

"Why are you staring at me like that?" His brows are raised. "Please stop."

His tone makes me laugh, and I jump at the opportunity to change the subject.

"You look like Thor, for heaven's sake. Thanks for doing yourself up tonight."

"Doing myself." I can hear his chuckle over the sound

of the music. "Sounds about right."

"You're so immature."

"You're *so* welcome."

"That wasn't a compliment, Kip." My eyes land on the royal blue hair band around his topknot. "How the hell did you get your hands on a scrunchie?"

"My sister is an asshole and sent me a box of them, okay? Because of my man buns." He fingers the scrunchie in his mop. "I thought this crushed velvet one suited the occasion nicely."

"First of all, how do you know that's crushed vel—you know what? Never mind." I squint up at him. "What's the occasion?"

"Our debut as a team."

"Jeez, please don't call it a debut. I predict this will be our one and only hurrah."

"It's a debut—unless you have a better word for it?"

"No, I don't." Frustrated, I throw my hands in the air. "Because we do not need to be calling it *any*thing! My god, why are you like this?"

Kip cocks a brow. "Okay, now you're starting to sound like my sister."

"Someone I bet I would really love from the sound of it. Tell me more."

"I'd really rather not. She's a pain in my ass."

"Is she tall?"

"I guess? Five ten or something."

"Whoa. Are you parents tall?"

"My dad is, not my mom."

"Hmm." I consider this. "So it's like a family of giants."

"Basically."

Just then, we're interrupted for the first time in an hour—since we've been here, it's just been the two of us entertaining ourselves with beer, banter, and small talk.

The guy is tall too—though not as tall as Kip—and handsome, in a pretty boy kind of way, a gash in his lip lending a rugged air. Hair tussled, he's got on a button-down shirt, sleeves rolled to the elbow, and jeans that look like they could stand to go through the wash.

"Hey Sasquatch. What's up?" He gives me side eye and a smile, holding up two red cups.

"Not much, Lynwood." Kip steps forward, inching farther into what's supposed to be a three-foot chasm, chest bumping my back.

I step away.

He follows.

Dammit!

"Who's your friend?" the guy asks.

"This is Teddy."

Lynwood smiles. "Like the bear?"

"No, dipshit." Kip is already irritated, and his friend has only been standing here for about seven seconds. "Like the name."

Oh lord.

Lynwood ignores Kip, turning to me; giving me all his attention. It's weird, in a way, his brown eyes shining a little too bright. His smile a little too wide. Wolflike.

I don't think I trust him.

"Teddy, I'm Steve."

I shyly brush a lock of hair behind my ear. "Hi."

"*Jesus*," I hear Kip grunt, and I want to elbow him in the abs—then I remember rule seven. I'm not allowed to punch him in the gut. Crap.

I need him to stop acting like a dick.

"You thirsty, Teddy?"

I hand Kip the cup in my hand and return my gaze to Steve. "Sure."

He hands me one of the two red cups he brought over.

"Thanks." I go to put it to my smiling mouth. Aww, how thoughtful of him to bring me a drink.

But it's yanked out of my hand and away from my lips.

"What the hell, Kip?" He is such a savage.

"Give me that."

He plucks the cup from my grasp, hands it back to Steve, and then looks down his nose at me.

Sniffs indignantly before flaring his nostrils. "Rule number eighty that *every*fucking*body* knows: never accept beer from a dude handing it to you at a party. Ever. It could have drugs in it."

My brows shoot up—I hadn't thought of that. Then again, Kip has been with me most of the night and I haven't had to. He's the best watchdog a girl could have.

Steven's lip curls up. "What the hell, Carmichael?"

"I'm not saying you drugged her, dipshit—I'm talking generalities." Kip side-eyes Steven, shooting me a pointed look. "But still, I mean…he *could* have."

"You are so unbelievably fucked up, man." Steve huffs.

"What-the-fuck-*ever*, dude—she should know better."

"You're an asshole."

The curse words keep coming as they begin to argue, in the middle of the living room, for the entire party to see.

"Piss *off*, Lynwood."

This sure escalated quickly.

"You think you're tough shit because you're ten feet tall, but you ain't shit."

Kip's nostrils flare. "How about you walk away—she's too good for you anyway."

"Fuckin' A, Carmichael. I wasn't even interested in her to begin with. Look at her, Jesus—she looks like a kindergarten teacher."

Wait—what does *that* mean? Did he just imply that I was *homely*? My mouth drops open—I've never been insulted to my face before.

"What did you just say?" Kip moves forward, chest practically bumping Lynwood's if not for their drastic height difference. "How about you watch your fucking mouth."

"I'll say whatever the hell I want, you giant freak."

"Get the fuck out of my face," Kip thunders.

"Not a problem, asshole."

Kip rolls his eyes, tired of the conversation, appearing so bored I expect him to check his fingernails. "You called me an asshole already, you asshole."

Steve storms off, weaving his way back through the crowd, and I watch his brown head bobbing above the throng until it disappears from sight.

"What. Just. Happened?"

"Not worth your time. He's an idiot."

Obviously.

I clear my throat, trying to appear unruffled and unaffected, even though Steve Lynwood's drunk, biting words will haunt me the remainder of the evening: *I wasn't even interested in her to begin with. Look at her, Jesus.*

What the hell did he mean by that?

"Okay, well he's the third idiot you've scared away tonight."

"Uh, yeah, because they're *all* fucking idiots."

"I'm sure not *all* of them are…"

"Nope. They are."

"Including you?"

"Especially me." Kip lifts the red cup in his hands, putting it to his lips. I watch his throat constrict as he swallows then lowers it, crushing the entire thing in his giant claw. "This party blows, and so do these guys."

I rub my chin, tapping it. "There's a blowjob joke in there somewhere."

"Please don't make it—the last thing we need is me thinking about you giving blowjobs."

"If you knew this party was going to *blow* then why are we here?"

"We're here because you need practice."

"Or, I can just find a nice guy in one of my labs, because this…apparently this is not my scene."

"*Or* you broaden your dating pool by swimming outside the dork pond."

"Stereotype much?"

"Yes. Don't you?"

I scoff. "Pfft, no."

"Liar—you stereotyped me."

"Well…how could I not? Look at you—you look like Bigfoot's cousin."

"Bigfoot isn't a real person, Theodora."

"But if he *was*—"

"He's not."

"For the sake of argument—"

"He's not though, so we can't argue about it."

"Kipling, I swear on all that is holy—"

This agreement is never going to work, and why on earth I thought it would is completely lost on me.

I open my mouth and tell him, "You're fired."

"*What?*"

"This isn't going to work. You're too confrontational, and you're not going to like *any*one who talks to me—plus none of these guys are my type. So you're fired."

"I'm free labor—you can't fire me."

"So we agree this isn't working? And that we're done."

"Fine. Can we just stop arguing now and go to my house?"

He wants to leave? Fine by me, I've spoken to almost no guys anyway, haven't had the chance to flirt, and haven't seen my friends all night, either.

I'm exhausted.

"You want me to come over?" I can't hide the surprise in my voice. He wants me to go to his place—again? I thought he didn't like people there.

He gives me a wide-shouldered shrug. "Sure, why not. You already know where I live—not that I want you dropping by unexpectedly."

As if I'd do that. "Like I'd be able to find it on my own."

"Whatever. Just get your shit and let's bounce. This party sucks but I'm not tired. We can watch a movie or play a game or something."

Play a game?

"Yeah okay, I could do a movie. And we can leave now, because I didn't bring any shit. I could stand to run home to grab some sweats, though."

Kip jingles his glittery car keys. "Sure."

"Then let's go."

I can text Mariah later to let her know I'm not staying.

To be honest, she won't even notice I'm gone.

***

KIP

Ronnie: *Doing*

Kip: Why do you do that?

Ronnie: Do what?

Kip: Ask what I'm doing by only using that one word. It's so freaking annoying.

Ronnie: I know LOL

Ronnie: So? What are you doing?

Kip: Why?

Ronnie: Can't I check in on you?

Kip: It's midnight on a Friday—what do you think I'm doing?

Ronnie: I know what you're NOT doing—a GIRL HAHAHAHA

Kip: You're funny.

Ronnie: Hey, speaking of girls—what happened with that stray you brought home last weekend?

Kip: Teddy isn't a stray. And right now she's in the bathroom peeing.

Ronnie: Whose bathroom?

Kip: Mine.

Ronnie: SHUT UP. SHE IS NOT IN YOUR HOUSE AGAIN??? What?! Stop it.

Ronnie: WHY? Who is this girl and what has she done to you?

Kip: Knock it off.

Ronnie: CLEARLY she has a magic vagina.

Kip: I wouldn't know.

Ronnie: SHUT. UP. Two weekends in a row and you haven't slept with her? You have issues, you know that right?

Kip: Yes, I know that.

Ronnie: So you put her in the friend zone? Is she cool with that?

Kip: Trust me, she's not into me.

Ronnie: Hmm, are you sure?

Kip: She changed out of the dress she wore to the party and into a cow onesie. It's really unflattering.

Ronnie: Oh. Seriously?

Kip: No. But trust me, she's not into me.

Ronnie: Did she invite herself over or did you invite her over?

Kip: I invited her.

Ronnie: Okay...

Ronnie: Why would you do that?

Kip: I don't fucking know, Ron—to watch movies? That's what people do with their friends.

Ronnie: At midnight on a Friday. Because you always invite your "friends" to the house. Righhhht...

Kip: That's what normal people do, Ronnie. They have friends over.

Ronnie: NEWSFLASH KID: You are not "normal people" and you don't ever have people over to your house. Does she think it's weird you're not living in a shithole?

Kip: I think so, but she's been cool about it. She doesn't gush over it or anything.

Ronnie: Well that's good.

Ronnie: Does she know what you look like without all the hair? Has she seen any photos lying around?

Kip: There are no pictures lying around, give me a damn break.

Ronnie: So she has no idea how cute you are?

Kip: How do I respond to that? No, I guess Teddy doesn't know what I look like without the hair—and she's not going to.

Ronnie: Hairy beast mode.

Kip: Yup.

Ronnie: Suit yourself, baby brother.

Kip: I will.

Ronnie: Still not getting any action, either, are you? Still celibate as a monk?

Kip: None LOL

Kip: TTYL she's coming.

Ronnie: Coming! Get it! But not from you though…

Kip: **eye roll** Go to sleep.

***

"Why is it so damn cold in here? Kip, I'm freezing!"

"The furnace went out last night and I haven't gotten anyone to come fix it yet." I would think that was obvious—it's not like I'm purposely living in a cold house. "Did I forget to mention that?"

"Yes! You forgot to mention your house was sixty degrees!"

"Huh. Well, whatever—put on a sweatshirt."

"You invited me over to your place knowing it was an ice box? Thanks so much."

"Relax! *Relax*. I'm going to try to fix it myself in the morning."

"But it's cold right *now*."

"But it won't be in the morning."

Her raised brow conveys her skepticism. "Do you even know how to fix a furnace?"

Hell no.

"It's called YouTube—ever heard of it? I'll watch a tutorial like everyone else on the planet. How hard could it be?"

Her scowl deepens. "Do you really think fixing it yourself is a good idea?"

"It's worth a shot before I call someone." I toss my jacket on the chair in the kitchen and bend to untie my boots.

Teddy does the same, unzipping the gold zippers going down the back of her black boots.

"Far be it from me to judge. You look like you might know your way around a woodshed, but not a toolbox. After seeing you in your natural habitat—white marble tile and high-end everything, I'm not so sure you can fix it yourself. No offense."

I pause to look up. "What's that supposed to mean?"

"I mean…I'm sensing you haven't really had to lift a finger growing up."

Obviously she's correct—I didn't have to lift a finger growing up. We had cooks and gardeners and maintenance crew to do those things for us. We had a cleaning staff, tutors, and…

In a nutshell, my parents weren't doing my sister or me any favors preparing us for the real world—something I've grown to resent. I can't even fucking fix a furnace, or unclog a toilet at two in the morning (another thing I had to google), or use a Skilsaw when I wanted to build a shelf in the spare room I use as an office.

I stand, crossing my arms, affronted. "Based on *what*?"

Her eyes dart around the room then land on the expensive faux fur throw blankets draped over the back of my couch. My mother bought them for me.

"Um…" Teddy bites her bottom lip. "Based on the fact that you probably have a cleaning lady. I bet someone does your laundry *and* grocery shopping."

"I do my own grocery shopping." Most of the time.

"But you have a cleaning lady?"

My lips pull into a tight line.

"Oh my god, stop it. You do not!" Teddy practically shouts into the otherwise silent room. "Do you? *Stop*. Do you?"

My cheeks flush; I can feel the heat rising up my neck, suddenly embarrassed by my privilege.

"Yes," I grind out. "Can we not talk about it?"

Another long stretch of silence follows—and for a bit, I think she is going to say something more about it. Am pleasantly surprised when she doesn't. Relieved, actually, when instead she laughs and says, "That would explain why there is no pee around your toilet bowl."

I pee mostly in the toilet, thank you very much miss know-it-all.

I walk farther into the living room, knowing she's going to trail behind after me. "I can totally take you home if you don't think you can hack it in this cold house."

She glances down at the leggings and hooded sweatshirt she changed into when we got home. Pulls at the thick material and huffs. "I don't have anything on underneath—no layers, and these leggings are thin. I think I might actually die."

"It's called a blanket." I lean forward, nabbing one of the fancy throws from the end of the couch, toss it at her. "Use it."

Teddy huffs again when it pelts her in the face, throwing herself into the corner of the couch. "Fine, I'll stay."

"I can take you home if it's going to be a problem," I say firmly, repeating the offer.

"No, no, I'll get over it. Just let me be super dramatic about it for a few more seconds—then I'll drop the subject."

I plop down next to her and palm the remote control, pointing it at the television while she sighs and squirms on the cushions next to me, making a bit of a racket, trying to get comfortable. Makes one or two *brrr* sounds.

Shivers, finally settling on her ass, arms wrapped around her legs.

The look I shoot her is one of exasperation. "You're ridiculous."

"I have a few more seconds, remember? Let me be."

I grin, shaking my head. Fuck she's sweet.

I jump when she uncurls, her feet sliding across the couch cushions in my direction, moving under the blankets like a snake, icy skin grazing mine and making me yelp.

"Get your cold feet off of me! Warn a person, *Christ*."

Teddy laughs. "Let me stick them under your thighs. Please? They're frozen."

I can feel her wiggling them before she pokes my thigh with her big toe.

"Jesus, you should go to the doctor and have that checked out."

"Shut up." She laughs. "They're not that bad."

"Yes they are." They really are—cold, that is, and they're cooling down my mesh athletic pants where she's brazenly slid them under my leg. "You clearly have poor circulation."

"I do not." She doesn't sound concerned, not one bit.

"First thing Monday morning, I'm taking you to the clinic."

I love hearing her laugh. I love the way her feet are tucked under my legs, body stretched out next to mine, our size difference conspicuous. But nice.

I might be a goddamn giant compared to her, but hell if I don't feel protective because of it.

We stay like this for over an hour, wrapped up in furry blankets, talking through the movie, chatting and laughing until we're both yawning.

"I don't know if I'm tired or suffering from hypothermia," she quips, dragging the blanket to her chin.

"Both. Definitely both," I tease, admiring the bridge of her nose backlit by the kitchen light. It slopes gently, the tip of it pert. Cute.

The bow of her lips, bottom one full.

Wisps of hair, gathered up into a topknot just like mine—yeah, we fucking match—some falling out in messy disarray.

She doesn't give a shit what she looks like in front of me, doesn't care because she's comfortable.

When her head tips back onto the couch, her cheek

hits my shoulder and I catch her giving me a sniff. Catch her biting down on her bottom lip, head lifting and turning away.

Busted.

Okay, maybe not so comfortable with me after all.

No fucking way is she attracted to me; I would know.

Wouldn't I?

Guys know this shit, and she's definitely not interested. Her speed is more the science dorks and history geeks, lab rats and guys with middle-class parents who fish and play kickball on the weekends.

I don't do any of that shit.

Teddy would shit a solid gold brick if she knew where I grew up and what we did for fun on the weekends, and it sure as hell wasn't kickball.

Still…

I can't help imagining what dating her would be like.

Nice.

Normal.

God, normal—what's that even like?

I've been trying to figure that shit out for the past couple years, starting with my move from Notre Dame back to Bumblefuck, Iowa. This house I could do nothing about; my parents insisted on a place where they could install a security system in a safe, discreet neighborhood, a place where reporters and all that other bullshit weren't likely to look for me.

For a story.

My sister has managed some normalcy in her personal

life, marrying a dude she met on a dating app instead of one of the men my parents tried setting her up with—guys they'd hoped would help expand their empire.

Ronnie moved clear across the country to a small town, population three thousand. Bought a house on a lake, doing it all herself. Raising her own kids, doing her own laundry. Regular shit.

Normal shit.

The shit that I want, if even for a while.

I pluck at a strand of Teddy's hair—the curly tendril falling to her shoulder, rubbing it between my thumb and middle finger.

I expect her to pull away and ask what the *hell* it is I think I'm doing, but for whatever reason, she lets me play with her hair. Watches me, a sleepy half-smile on her face.

Man she's pretty.

***

"Teddy...you awake?"

A loud gasp comes out of the dark, from the general area of the bed, and when I flip the hall light on, I find Teddy sitting straight up, squinting toward the hallway, shielding her eyes.

"Dammit, Kip! Did you have to sneak up on me like that? You scared me half to death and jeez, turn the damn light off! You're freaking blinding me!"

She sure is feisty when she's woken up.

I lean against the doorjamb. "I'm six foot four—it's humanly impossible for me to sneak up on anyone."

"Bigfoot can sneak up on anyone he wants to sneak up

on," she grumbles, trying to burrow deeper into the pillows. "No one has caught him yet."

"He's not real."

A finger flies into the air, pointed in my general direction. "Do *not* start that crap with me right now or I will *kill* you."

"Just sayin', I prefer the name Sasquatch if it's all the same to you."

"*Why* are you like th—" Her words cut off. "God, listen to us. It's…what the hell time is it?" She leans toward the table next to the bed, fumbling for her phone. "One o'clock. We've only been in bed for half an hour—what's going on? Why are you in here? Is the house on fire? Is the heat working again?"

"No."

"Well—what then?" The blanket clutched to her chest gets pulled to her chin.

"Are you doin' okay?"

"No, Kip. I'm f-freezing my ass off is what I'm *doin'*." She mimics my tone. Far be it from me to point out: that is not how I sound.

"I can't sleep either. You want me to take you home so you can sleep?"

She squints at me impatiently, shielding the light from her eyes with one hand. "Kip, it is one o'clock in the morning. By the time I get home and settle in, it'll be two. I'll tough it out—I've been camping in colder weather than this."

"Camping in a *tent*?"

The look she shoots me is one of pure disgust. "What

other kind of camping is there?"

"I wouldn't know."

She sits up. "You've never been camping? Wow. Considering you look like a yeti, I am somewhat shocked by this news. What else haven't you done?"

"Can we have this conversation in my room? I'm fucking cold."

"Like…in your bed?" Pause. "Why?"

"It has a better mattress and a thicker comforter." Do I really need to explain this? "Come on, I'm freezing. The body heat will keep us warm."

"Did you read that somewhere in a survival guide? 'Cause we know you're not outdoorsy. You only wear plaid to throw people off."

"Very funny, smartass." But also true. "Get up—come on."

I give the blanket on her bed a hard yank so it flies off, landing in a heap at my feet, forcing her out of the bed. Haul her covers down the hallway toward my room, the sound of her screeching echoing after me.

"What the hell is wrong with you? Give me back that blanket—I'm not wearing any pants!"

Now I'm the one who's disgruntled. "You're cold so you took off your leggings? Where's the logic in that?"

"Stop talking before I murder you!"

She is so loud when she's fired up. "I don't feel sorry for you anymore. Throw your leggings back on and come warm me up."

"I hate you right now."

"No you don't—admit it, you're relieved I came to rescue you."

"This is stupid," she bickers, dragging her feet across the threshold to my room. "We could have gone to my apartment and actually had a decent night's sleep."

Pfft. "And risk the chance of molestation by Mariah? No thanks. I'd rather freeze my testicles off."

Besides, no way would I fit in her bed. Or on her couch.

Her laughter rings out, accenting the sound of her bare feet padding toward my room across the carpet. "That sounds like a definite possibility."

I toss the extra comforter atop mine and whip back the covers, climbing into my side while she hobbles down the hallway corridor, hopping into her tight bottoms.

Struggle bus, jeez.

"Hurry up, dude."

I'm almost positive she's glaring daggers in my direction. "You did not just call me dude."

"I did. Climb in, slowpoke."

"Hold your horses—your bed is like, five feet off the ground. I can't deal with this at one in the morning." I watch in the shadows, across the mattress, as Teddy attempts to hoist herself off the ground, up onto my California king. "This is way too much work."

"I'm tall—what did you expect? A mini twin?"

"No, but…maybe. I don't know anyone with a bed like this."

"Then you should get out more."

She finally makes it up, sliding in under the covers and

pulls them over her body, leggings back in place, toes rooting their way around underneath the sheets.

In my direction.

"Please don't touch me with those," I warn.

"Why?" She sounds whiney. "You let me do it before on the couch."

"Because you're a brute and made me let you."

"They'll warm up in no time if you let me just…" I feel her toes hit the side of my calf muscle.

I pull it back. "This isn't a slumber party, Theodora."

"You think this is what girls do at slumber parties? Tickle each other with their toes?" She laughs. "You are so far off. Besides, I wouldn't be in here if you had heat. So this is your fault."

True. "What do girls do at slumber parties?"

"Uh…talk about boys, eat, and watch chick flicks, mostly."

"That sounds really fucking boring."

Another musical little laugh comes trilling out of the dark. "Whatever, Kip. Let me stick my feet under you."

"No way. Get away." My protests are getting weak, mostly because it's her, and I find her pretty fucking adorable.

"Well then move closer—you said you were going to share body heat with me. Don't be a liar, Kipling."

I haven't been in bed with or lain next to a girl in—I do a mental tally of the weeks, months—years. A long fucking time is what it adds up to, and I can't stop my body from reacting to Teddy being under my covers. Smelling her perfume. Breathing the same air. Wanting to share heat.

Body heat.

Shit, this was my dumb idea—what the hell was I thinking?

I wasn't.

I didn't expect this to be a big deal. Share blankets, stay warm—simple, easy. Any idiot could do this without a problem.

I should be able to do this without a problem; I've been keeping people at a distance for *years*. I friend-zoned Teddy within seconds of meeting her, and she has no interest in me, either.

Except…

Maybe I've been fooling myself.

Maybe I'm not as immune to women as I thought I was. Or maybe I'm just not immune to Teddy Johnson— sweet, beautiful, naïve Teddy.

Maybe I knew as soon as I saw her at that first party that we'd end up here. *Because she's different.*

She yawns beside me, nestling her toes deeper into the crux of my bent legs, their temperature having climbed twofold.

I don't exactly hate it.

"You don't think it's weird that we're in bed together?" Her question comes out of nowhere.

"Why would I think it's weird?"

"Uh, because it's weird? We're not even friends—not really. And we're not dating, but you have this weird…" Pause. "I know you're protective of me, and I can't figure out why, but I also know I don't hate it, either. It's…nice."

Right.

"I just didn't think I'd ever be in some guy's bed platonically, that's all. College guys are such pigs sometimes."

"I'm not a pig."

"I know you're not—that's what I'm saying. Sometimes it's confusing. You're not gay, but you don't date, and you're not sleeping with anyone. You must spend a lot of time…*you know*."

The word she's looking for here is masturbating.

"Don't *you*?" I'm curious. "Spend time doing that?"

"No!" She's shocked.

"*Why*?"

"I don't know how? God, Kip." The answer—which is in the form of a both a question and a confession—comes out halted. "I can't believe I just said that. I must be delirious."

The air around us crackles. Kip bolts upright, twisting his body toward me.

"What do you mean, *you don't know how*? Everyone knows how—you put your hand down your pants, move it around, and boom, orgasm." Sounds like she needs a tutorial of Masturbating for Dummies.

"I don't think it's that simple." She giggles, patronizing me.

"Oh, but Teddy, it is. It really, really is that simple."

"Yeah, probably because you've been jerking off since you were like twelve, and all you really have to do is move your hand up and down on your penis. There's barely any work involved."

No comment.

Suddenly I twist my body to face her, bending my elbow and propping myself up in her direction. "So let me get this straight—you've never touched yourself?"

"Of course I've touched myself."

I roll my eyes. "The shower to get clean doesn't count."

"Oh."

"*Oh*, she says," I tease. "You're really missing out if you're not rubbing one out a few times a week."

She groans, embarrassed. "Rubbing one out? That's one I haven't heard before."

"It's all part of self-love, Teddy."

"And I bet you love yourself a whole lot," comes her low chuckle.

She has no idea.

"Why do you even care?" she asks.

"I don't. You're the one who brought it up—I'm just the one who ran with it."

"Actually, I *didn't*."

"Yes you did. You were all"—my speech gets high-pitched as I mimic her girl voice—"*You must spend a lot of time blah blah blah…you know.*"

"I do not sound like that." In the dark, I hear her eyes roll.

"But you *did* say it."

"Fine. I'm curious, all right? Sue me. You're this giant of a guy, who must be—"

She stops herself.

"Spit it out, Teddy. Stop hesitating." It's driving me nuts!

"Fine! You're this giant of a guy who must get...*excited* a lot. There, happy now?"

"And by excited you mean..."

"Horny, okay?" The words burst out of her. "Thank god it's dark, my face is on fire."

Yup. I made her say the word horny, and she sounds horrified, and it's perfect.

"And you're not? Horny?"

"*Uh*...when would I have the time? And please stop saying that word—it's awful. It's worst than the word moist. Or squirt."

She hates the word moist? What's wrong with the word moist?

"You hate horny? You don't have time to be horny?" I say it again, twice, just to embarrass her. "You're shitting me, right? Everyone has time to be horny. What the hell is wrong with you?"

"It's perfectly normal not to be turned on all the time."

"No. It's not." At least, I don't think it is.

"How would you even know? You're not a female."

"No, but I've seen enough of them around campus and at parties to know most are sex-crazed lunatics."

"Are you *high* right now?" she barks at me through the shadows. "Who are you hanging out with? Absolutely no one is running around campus like a sex-crazed lunatic, except maybe the guys."

"False. *I* am not a sex-crazed lunatic."

"What are you then? Because I doubt you're a virgin."

Definitely not a virgin. "No. I just swore off girls when they became too much trouble."

"Trouble? How?"

"You know, wanting to get serious and shit."

"Ah, so you're one of thoooose." She drags the word out, as if she's finally cracked my code, satisfaction lacing every syllable. "A commitment-phobe."

"You wouldn't understand."

"Pfft. Try me."

"Nope. We are not having this conversation." Especially not in the middle of the night.

"Oh, but we *are*." If we were seated at a table, she'd be crossing her arms and leaning back, waiting for my reply like a boss. Giving me the stink eye. Puffing on a cigar, killing me with silence.

"Let's just agree to disagree, okay? I don't need to justify why I'm not into dating, and you don't need to justify why you don't like touching yourself downtown."

"Oh my god."

I uncurl myself, rolling to my back, gaze staring up at the ceiling in the pitch black.

"I have a question for you: what if I like it so much I never want to have sex with a guy?"

"What if you love *jerking yourself off* so much you never want to have sex with a dude? I don't even know how to respond to that, Teddy."

The thought is inconceivable.

"But that's what happened to you, right? You masturbated yourself single. You don't *need* a female. You have two hands to keep you satisfied."

There's probably an element of truth to that, but, "Sometimes it's not enough."

Jesus. Why did I admit that out loud?

"I could have told you that, and I'm not even doing it. You can't replace *real* intimacy, Kip, no matter how hard you try."

"Thanks, *Mom*. I'll keep that in mind."

Teddy only gives me a few seconds of reprieve before she hits me with her next assault. "Why don't you like having people over?"

I sigh, long and loudly into the dark, tucking my arms behind my head. "Who said I don't like having people over?"

I feel her shrug when the mattress dips, though I can't see it.

"I just assumed since you *never* have people over." She pauses, uncertain. "Is it because you're embarrassed?"

Is she serious? "Embarrassed about what?"

"That you...that your..." She falters, searching for the right words.

I wait her out.

"It's pretty obvious you come from money, okay?"

Teddy has *no* idea.

"I don't think you should be ashamed of it," she goes on in the dark.

"I'm not."

"Whatever you say, Kipling Carmichael." Teddy laughs, wiggling her feet. They're dainty, and small, and feel good still tucked beneath me. "God, even that name sounds…rich, like you should be on a yacht somewhere in the Pacific."

The Atlantic, actually. That's where the boat is docked, at some marina with a yacht club, near one of several Carmichael vacation homes.

"It's not a crime coming from money, just like it's not a crime for me to be—I don't know, poor, I guess. A scholarship kid. I'm not ashamed, though I used to be. Not anymore. I work my ass off, and so does my mom."

Her body shivers.

"You can move over a little if you're still cold." I know I am. My nuts are shriveled up, practically ascended into my body.

"No funny business."

As if.

"Just scoot your ass over here."

"Okay, okay. So *bossy*."

Teddy's feet pull out from under me and soon the heat from her flat stomach, from between her legs, and from her tits are burning my skin where she's pressed up against me.

Goddamn. When I told her to scoot over, I didn't mean *Singe me with all your best parts.* How the fuck am I supposed to sleep with the apex of her thighs straddling my hip?

Next, she throws her arm over my chest, fingers casually resting on the bicep opposite, hand falling limp.

"Oh my god, you are so warm! This feels so amazing."

She hunkers down closer, squeezing me. "Mmm, heaven."

Her long, dark hair tickles my nostrils, and I draw in a breath to sniff it as discretely as I can.

Clean and fruity and I want to bury my nose in it.

And my hands.

Those lie limply at my sides, one buried beneath her, the other on the mattress—

"Your beard tickles."

"So does your hair." Hair I'm tempted to sink my fingers into, to test its weight and feel how soft it is.

We lie like this for who knows how long, my chest heaving up and down, heart rate accelerated like I've just run a mile. I wonder if she can hear it beating—if she knows she's the reason it's racing.

"I've never been this comfortable in my entire life." She sighs, content. "I could lie like this every night."

"Only because your survival instincts kicked in."

"Or because you're like a giant teddy bear."

Suddenly, Teddy pulls away. In the shadow of the moon shining through the window, I watch her sit up and pull the fabric of her sweatshirt up and over her head, tossing it to the end of the bed.

What's left is the silhouette of her breasts veiled in a thin T-shirt, and when she lies back down beside me, the hard peaks of her nipples graze my ribcage.

"It's warm enough under these covers I don't need that anymore."

She settles back in, curling into my side, really making herself at home against my body. Hikes her leg over my thigh, the warmest parts of her boiling my skin.

"Mmm."

I can literally feel the fucking heat from her pussy against my leg.

"Whoa, whoa, whoa—what the hell do you think you're doing?"

What I should do is shove her off the bed, onto the floor, and get the fuck out of my own room. Fast.

She pats me on the chest, her touch more of a caress than a chastising reprimand.

"Relax! You're like one of those pregnancy body pillows I've seen in Target. Stop moving around so much or you're going to mess up my positioning."

A pregnancy body pillow? What the fuck is she talking about?

I can't concentrate when her delicate hand, which was previously resting innocently on my arm, begins to wander, finger trailing over my left pec, hand pressing into my skin. Poking. Kneading at my muscles.

"Could your body *be* any harder?"

Yup.

Yes, I can be harder.

Keep that shit up and you'll find out just how hard I can be.

"Jeez, Kip—how often do you work out? All day, every day?"

"Please stop."

Poke.

Poke.

"Teddy, stop."

"Oh please—you're immune to me, remember?"

I'm only immune to you when your perky set of amazing tits isn't pressed against my body in the middle of the fucking night, reminding me how fucking long it's been since I've boned someone.

"I never said I was immune to you, Teddy. I said I wasn't dating anyone or having sex."

"And *I* said I was curious. It's harmless, I'm not going to try anything—I wouldn't even know how."

That does not make me feel any better; in fact, that makes this whole thing worse, because now all I'm thinking about is being the one who can teach her...*stuff.*

"Did you know I haven't ever seen a guy this close up before? I want to take advantage of the opportunity—since it's you."

A few things hit me at once. One, she doesn't realize touching me, roaming her hands all over my body is going to eventually make me hard.

And two: Teddy just admitted she's a virgin.

My brain kicks into overdrive, reacting to the soft glide of her palm over my cotton T-shirt. The path it takes down the center of my ab muscles, pausing when they involuntarily contract. Flex. Tighten.

Oh shit.

Ohhh. Shit.

"Wow, I knew you were ripped, but these are..." Her voice is low, full of wonder, the hum inside her throat one of appreciation. "Ridiculous."

She makes another little sound of pleasure.

I don't know what to fucking do—take her hand off me and tell her to respect my boundaries? Do us both a favor and roll away, creating distance?

Or let her explore and see where those curious fingers roam next?

Inside my mesh athletic bottoms, my dick stirs.

Twitches.

"You really are a gentleman, Kip."

"I'm really not."

She has no idea.

It stretches toward the fabric, alerted to the presence of a foreign hand, to the soothing female voice not far from my ear.

"Uh huh." Her arms snakes around my middle, hugging me, body pressed so tightly against mine it's as if we were one person. "Your skin is so warm. God you feel good."

God you feel good?

Those are sex words, those are sex words, my body screams, even though Teddy isn't being sexual—is she?

Nope. She's snuggling me, for fuck's sake.

Unless she's not?

No, she definitely is.

Or maybe she's not?

Shit, shit, fuck my life.

"Why are you so tense right now?" Comes a low, soothing voice. "Should I rub your back?"

"Jesus no!" I shout. "I mean—no thanks, I'm good."

"You really must be tired, 'cause you're so grouchy all of a sudden. Close your eyes and I'll rub your shoulders."

As she lies next to me, her innocent hands are already there, slowly rubbing circles over my collarbone, clavicle, and deltoid. Goddamn, it feels good.

Still…

"Please don't."

"Mmm, why not?"

"Because…" *Because you just went Mmm, and it made my dick stiffen up, that's why not.* Does she really not get it? Or is she playing dumb? She can't be this clueless.

Can she?

"Just relax, okay?"

"That's not gonna happen." I bark out a laugh, wanting to move away but paralyzed.

Her fingers brush the bottom of my beard then lightly caress my cheeks.

"Your skin is so soft where you don't have hair—too bad there isn't much of it showing."

"Yup, just how I like it."

"You know what girls always talk about when they see a guy with a beard?"

"How repulsive it is?"

"Uh, *no.*" Teddy laughs. "They talk about what it would feel like between their legs."

"*What?*" Another laugh from her and I'm ready to fly off the damn bed. "You're lying."

"Did you not know that?"

"No."

"Kip, they make T-shirts that say *Bearded for her pleasure*. You should get one—I'd get you one myself, but I'm broke, ha."

"Wait—*what*?"

"Have you been living under a rock? Beards are so trendy right now. Even *I* know that, and I'm the untrendiest person I know. That doesn't mean I like beards, but everyone else does—girls, I mean."

That would explain so many things: girls still approaching me at parties, wanting to touch my beard. Touching my mustache at the bar. Making lewd comments. Telling me I should enter contests.

I always thought they were joking. Shit, maybe I have been living under a rock—otherwise known as the Midwest.

Teddy drones on, fingers at the base of my neck, kneading at a knot. "...and I saw a girl wearing one that said *My other ride is a beard*. Get it?"

She says it so casually, yet the sudden image of her sitting on my face while I suck on her—

Her throat gives a little mew, fingers still massaging my sensitive skin. "You've heard of a beardgasm before, haven't you?"

"Stop."

Her fingers stop.

"I didn't mean you had to stop doing *that*, I meant stop saying shit like that, about beards and orgasms and crap."

"Why?" She sounds about as perplexed as I'm feeling right now. "We're just talking."

"Because it's getting me hard." Er. Hard-*er*.

There. If that doesn't scare her off, nothing will.

Seconds of silence pass.

Then minutes.

"*Is* it?" Her voice is barely a whisper. Fascinated.

"Yes." Mine is gruff.

"Why?"

"Why?" I deadpan. "Because I'm in bed with a pretty girl, in the middle of the fucking dark, and her hand is on my body—one that hasn't been touched in years, by the way. And you're going on and *fucking on* about oral." I pause to take a breath. "That's why."

"Oh."

"Yeah, *oh*."

I lift my arm, hand searching for hers in the dark. Remove it from my shoulder, clasping her fingers. Place it back on my stomach, where it belongs—away from my chest and nipples and face.

Where I hope it will stay.

But apparently, I'm a fucking moron, because it doesn't.

Back and forth on my abs it goes.

Back.

Forth.

My hand—the hand lodged under Teddy's torso finally makes its way out, feeling along the cotton of her leggings. Lands on her ass.

Settles there, at least momentarily.

Back, her hand caresses.

And forth.

Until it meanders south, grazing the hemline of my shirt. Drifting back up inside it.

Skin on skin.

Palm against my tight abs.

"We should go to sleep." I sound so pitifully weak.

"We should." She agrees. Yawns.

Back.

And forth.

My cock throbs, the hand on her ass giving it a little squeeze. Then another, as the muscles in my thighs contract, because every single nerve ending throughout my entire fucking body is humming, alive and alert. Buzzing.

God I want her to touch it.

Fuck, just for a second, and then I can finish myself off in the bathroom.

Christ, what am I saying? I'm not going to jerk myself off with her in the house, as much as I want to.

If only she'd...

Just a little lower...

Please Teddy, please...

I count to ten—then ten again so my goddamn leg doesn't start bouncing like a jackrabbit's, tension-filled and nervous.

Slowly I take my hand, working it up her back. Underneath her shirt. Stroking the warm skin of her spine, fingers grazing her side boob. The tits pressed into my ribcage.

For fuck's sake, *please touch it.*

Graze it.

Flick it.

Anything.

Christ, I've never wanted anyone to touch my dick so bad. Or suck it, or stroke it, or…

Teddy says nothing when the pads of all five of my fingers brush her tender skin again. Only her sharp inhale of breath gives away the fact that she felt it. She holds that breath, waiting.

One second.

Two.

Four.

Five.

Her hand moves.

Down.

God, what is she doing? *What are we doing?* This is such a bad idea. I don't want her to stop.

That's it, Teddy. Lower. Lower. Oh fuck…

***

TEDDY

"That's it Teddy, lower…" Kip's low groan cuts into the dark, his guttural plea sexy and deep, hitting me right in the ovaries as he lays still beside me.

God, his voice. His words.

I doubt he realizes he's even saying them out loud.

Not Kip—he has too much self-control, and he's kept

me firmly at arm's length the past few weeks. There is no way he would purposely allow this to happen, unless…

Unless he really wanted me to. Or I was making him crazy, which I doubt, because—look at me. I'm the opposite of the girls who hang out at the rugby house. I'm wholesome and studious and, well, *virginal*.

The feel of Kip's hard, warm skin beneath my gliding fingertips is amazing. Warm, hot, and cool—all at the same time.

Him lying here motionless, allowing me to explore—it must be driving him insane; even I know that. I'm playing with fire and we both know it.

We should not be doing this.

Oh, who am I kidding? I'm the one with my hand practically down Kip's pants, running my palm along the happy trail I discovered under the soft fabric of his shirt.

I love those.

I think they're so sexy and masculine.

He obviously doesn't shave his junk like a lot of guys these days do. Metrosexuals.

His entire body stiffens when I skim the elastic waistband of his boxer briefs, trail a path with my hand, back and forth along the fabric. Teasing as I debate what the hell to do next.

One thing is for sure: I should not be doing this.

The thing is…I've never done *this* before. Not with a guy like this. They were boys, really, and it was mostly just making out and some heavy petting. Got fingered only once, in high school, with a kid named Devon, who was just as awkward as I was. Fumbling around in the dark with all our clothes on—two virgins who stayed that way—the closest I've gotten to having sex was him sticking his hand down my pants and shoving two fingers up my—

"Lower. Oh fuck, Teddy…"

My name on his lips.

It spurs me on, and suddenly, all I want to do is *touch* it. No harm in that, right? He obviously wants me to. Feel it. Maybe grip it, run my hand up and down its hard length (like I've seen in the few pornos I've snuck peeks at) just to see what it's like.

To hear what he sounds like when I do.

So I know.

I want to know what the other girls know, what it feels like to turn a guy on. What it feels like to make a dick hard. To make him come. The weight of a dick in my hands.

Yeah, that might sound gross, but I'm twenty-one and I have no clue what *it* feels like to hold one.

I don't want to be clueless anymore.

Kip seems to be a willing participant now that his dick is rock solid and my hand has somehow gotten wedged inside his boxers. He shifts his hips on the bed, gives a little thrust upward. Even without seeing them, I know he's flexing his thick thighs.

Ugh, those thighs *make me stupid.*

For weeks, I've been trying not to notice how they flex when he walks, how track pants and jeans don't quite fit properly because the muscles there bulge.

His giant, callused hand eases out from its spot under my body—I've been lying on it this entire time—and creeps to my ass. Palm splayed, fingers gripping my butt cheeks. Squeeze.

Leisurely, little by little, it makes its way up my back, under my shirt, slow circles along my spine. Up, up. *Down* under the thin cotton of my leggings, middle finger blazing a hot trail to my crack.

With my head on his chest and his beard flirting with the crown of my head, I finally snake my eager palm all the way inside his pants. It bumps the tip of his penis, its head straining against the layer of underwear, and I trace it with the tip of my finger. Run the pad of it round and round then go lower, feeling my way to the underside.

Trail along the shaft.

Entire palm closing over his...uh, *balls.*

Kip inhales again. Groans, fingers digging into my round butt cheeks. Breath coming hard and fast above me.

Timidly I stroke him through the material, not quite brave enough to stroke his actual...dick. Or touch it. Or—

I gasp when that thick finger of his that was grazing my rear is now firmly between my crack, easing its way to my pussy, causing my legs to ease apart.

"Get on top," he rumbles.

"Wha...?"

Swiftly, two arms are pulling me, rolling me, resting me on top, stiff erection cradled between my thighs. Large, masculine hands gripping my hips.

Pushing at my leggings.

"This would feel so much better if you pulled your pants down."

Wonderful idea.

Fantastic idea.

Two sets of arms and hands fumble to remove my leggings until they're low enough for me to kick off. Until I'm lying on top of Kip in nothing but a flimsy t-shirt and skimpy thong.

"Let's take yours off too," I hear myself say. Desperate to feel every inch of him without actually…feeling every inch of him.

I lift my hips as he shucks his track pants off, marveling at how intimate the whole thing is. We're not naked, but somehow we might as well be.

This is Kip, the guy who has become my friend in the past few weeks. The guy who has given me dating advice—albeit shitty, but advice nonetheless.

Kip, whose large, hairy body reaches for mine once his pants disappear into the bedroom. I hear them hit the floor somewhere in the distance at the same time his arms pull me down.

Line our bodies up like it's second nature.

Kip's hips begin a slow revolution until that dense, throbbing tip of him finds the fold between my legs and settles there.

"Oh my…fucking…*god.*" Kip exhales when his hands are back on my body, skimming gently over the globes of my butt. Over the back of my thighs. Up my shirt. Ribcage.

The sides of my breasts. Wanting to cup them but holding back.

"Can I touch them, Teddy? Just for a second?"

I want him to—so bad.

"Please." His plea is a whisper, a sexy, aching whim-

per.

"Okay." Yes, yes...!

"Sit up. Straddle me."

Kip adjusts himself on the mattress, taking me along with him, rising to a seated position. If we were naked, I'd be fully impaled on his cock.

I experiment, swiveling my hips.

He groans.

Grabs my shirt by the hem and lifts it all the way off.

In the dark, giant man paws find my shoulders, float their way down my biceps, then—

"Jesus, Teddy, your tits," he moans, palming them both, thumbs circling my stiff nipples. My mouth drops open as my head tips back, his lips and tongue flicking my skin. Mouth latching on and sucking, only coming up for air to say, "These are so perfect. I could suck on these all night."

"They're not perfect." My hands brace on his hard thighs for support as he continues to pull and draw my nipple into his greedy mouth. "You can't even see w-what they l-look like."

He lifts his head, beard scratching my chest. "I don't have to see these tits to know they're perfect, Teddy."

My arms go around his neck and I let him devour me, the throbbing between my legs unsatisfied. My lower half rakes back and forth over his dick, pushing and dragging and desperate for the tip to dig itself deeper into my pussy.

Somehow, our mouths fuse. Our first kiss, in the pitch black of his freezing cold bedroom, in the middle of the night—is frantic and hot and wet and dirty.

Tongues and lips and teeth. Beard scraping my face.

"Let me push your underwear to the side." His raspy tone is desperate. "It'll feel so good."

That's flirting with danger.

"Kip…" I might be protesting, but when his thumb reaches between us to push the barrier of my panties aside, we both sigh with relief. He was so right—it does feel amazing. So amazing, so amazing. Euphoric.

"I wanna be inside you so bad, fucking you." He pants, mimicking sex, pelvis gyrating, hands working my hips.

"No you don't. You're talking crazy."

"No, Teddy, I want to fuck you—I want to fuck you. I need to fuck you." He's repeating himself and sounds half crazed, nothing like I'm used to. He is losing control of the situation and dragging me down with him—except I'm all too eager to follow. I'm on top, dry humping him.

"Stop begging me, Kip." Before I lose control too.

"Let me eat you out, then, please."

Eat me out? Oh…

"Let me put my tongue inside your pussy, Teddy. Let me put my beard between your legs."

That has my attention. My full, undivided attention. My vagina's too, because it clenches at the thought, getting me hot all over again.

"Um…"

"Come on, baby—please. As long as it takes, just let me taste you."

"But, won't your beard get all…" Messy?

"Yes—fuck yeah it will."

K, well, that's kind of gross.

Still…

When he lifts me off him and lays me on my back, any protests die on my lips.

Kip's mammoth body eases down my petite one, shoulders nudging my legs apart.

A large finger draws down the center of my—

"NNNmm…" I gasp when the flick of a scorching tongue meets my clit. Presses firmly down. Mouth sucks. "Oh…god."

I have no idea what to do with myself right now, what to do with my arms, hands, body. Am I supposed to just lie here and let him…lick me like this? Do I move my hips around?

I feel so selfish letting him do all this work.

It's dark, so I can't see his head, but I can feel it—the messy mop top tickling my skin while his beard tickles my inner thighs.

Mustache and lips wreaking havoc on my clit.

My whole bottom half is going to have the equivalent of carpet burn, I just know it—but it'll be worth it.

I grasp at his shoulders as his elbows push against my knees, holding me open.

"You're so wet," he mumbles. "You taste so good— I'm going to be able to smell you for days."

Uh…thanks?

I try not to think about what I might smell like *down there*—I mean, I showered today, so that part is taken care of, right? But last night I had a fish sandwich for dinner, and *oh god, what am I even saying?*

Stop thinking and enjoy it, Teddy! Who knows when the next time is going to be that you'll have a chance like this. Mariah, Cameron, and Tessa are always bitching about how no one they date wants to go down on them, and here I am, legs spread while Kip goes to town on my...

Downtown.

He's groaning, and the sounds? Primal, as if we were actually having sex and he wasn't just performing oral.

Oral.

There is a guy with his head between my legs, and *it feels so good it feels so good it feels so*—"Uhh...uh..."

I can barely get any coherent words past my lips. Can't even be bothered to moan, my head thrashing on the pillow, fists clenched in his thick hair. Clenching the blankets. Clenching the pillow beneath my head.

Kip's tongue flattens, pushing deeper. Rolling. Licking. Sucking. And I swear, my legs quake.

"Come on baby. Come for me," he croons into the gap between my legs, the hair on his face doing crazy things to the nerves in my body, the soft yet coarse strands driving me *nuts.*

Jeez, how am I going to know if I'm coming or not? I've never done it, how could I possibly kn—

Yes, yes, that, right there!

That spot.

Keep doing that thing, that...that right th-there...

Everything inside me tightens and clenches and pulses and feels like heaven and, "Oh god, Kip, don't stop, don't stop whatever that is."

His voice is incoherent, his face—I imagine—entirely, thoroughly buried in my…in my…in…

When spasms rack the lower half of my body, I try to back away, push his head out, but he holds me down, continuing to suck the life of the orgasm from me.

Holy shit, holy mother of all that is holy.

I'm grateful for the dark, sure my mouth is hanging wide open when my head snaps back, my back arching.

Then, with a few casual licks against my sensitive nub, and a loud kiss to the middle, Kip releases my body.

I sag.

***

"You don't have to snuggle me now. It's okay."

His body wedges behind mine as soon as he crawls back up into bed after washing up, against my lifeless form, enveloping me. Hot, warm. Huge.

Kip's dick is still hard, pressed into the apex of my thighs, but he hasn't made any passes to remedy that, instead just letting it literally poke me in the ass.

"Maybe I want to."

His beard tickles the blades between my shoulders, and I shiver.

"Besides," he continues, "you'll freeze otherwise."

"I'm not cold." Not after that little show he just put on for me. On me.

"Not yet, but you're shivering."

"Kip, that isn't because I'm *cold.*"

"Oh." He laughs into my back, mouth and mustache

nuzzling the crook of my shoulder.

What the hell is going on? He's being all affectionate and sweet and we're spooning and now I'm confused. How did we get to this place?

I thought he hated shit like this.

I thought he didn't want anyone getting attached to him, and if that's the case, doing this with me is a terrible way to keep me at a distance.

"I'm sorry," I whisper into the dark, at the wall I'm facing.

"Why are you sorry?" His hand moves to stroke my hip.

"This was such a bad idea."

"No, actually, it was a really good idea." His heavy arm wraps around my middle, hand cupping my naked breast. Thumb traces my nipple.

"You're going to regret this in the morning."

"I promise you, Teddy, I won't."

Somehow, I don't believe him.

"But what if you want to do it all the time now, and it's my fault you broke your vow of celibacy?"

He pauses before speaking. "I didn't take a vow of celibacy. I just don't want to date or screw any catty, greedy bitc—*uh*, girls. I think my virtue is safe with you."

"Because I don't fall into those categories?"

"You definitely don't fall into those categories." My hair gets brushed to the side, and my eyes slide closed when his beard lands on my skin as he rests his chin. "My sister thinks so too."

What? He told his sister about me? "You told your sister about me?"

"I tell my sister everything."

He told his sister about me?

"What did you tell her?"

Kip yawns. "Just that you've been coming over. She's really protective, so…" His voice trails off, tired.

How am I going to sleep with his hot breath on my back? With his dick in my ass? With his broad chest heating my body like a damn furnace?

I've never slept in the same bed with a guy, never had one touch me like this before. The whole thing screams *Cozy! Domestic! Coupledom!*

Or maybe I'm delirious and have no idea what I'm talking about because I'm naïve and think the best of people and have no clue what I'm doing.

Honestly, I don't think Kip has any idea what he's doing, either.

And *that* makes it easier to fall asleep.

SECOND SATURDAY (BEFORE GAME)

"The morning I lose my damn mind and do something stupid, like fall for her..."

KIP

It's not as awkward in the kitchen with Teddy the next morning as I thought it was going to be.

I got up at the butt crack of dawn, before the sun and Teddy rose, and worked on the damn furnace for two hours. Seven YouTube videos and one service call later, the thing was up and running, warming the house to a blessed sixty-nine degrees.

Teddy is seated on a stool at the kitchen counter, blanket wrapped around her legs, clothes in place—many of them, as a matter of fact: hoodie, T-shirt peeking out of the bottom, and I'm guessing leggings covering those smooth legs.

Those legs.

I groan, remembering how it tasted between them:

fucking delicious.

Groan again, remember how I'm not fucking sleeping with girls.

But if I were, Teddy Johnson would be a great place to start.

She's adorable, blushing when I stroll into the room, dust on my jeans, black sweatshirt, and hands.

"Hey." My voice is gravelly. Low.

"Hey." She ducks her head, embarrassment flushing her cheeks. Teddy tucks a piece of hair behind her ear, even though she has it pulled up into a ponytail. It's still wavy and thick.

Damn, she's cute.

"Are you blushing?"

"Um…no."

"Yeah you are—you should see how ruddy your skin is."

She turns to face me, coffee cup in hand, eyes in gorgeous, narrow slits. Should I not have called her complexion ruddy?

"No, Kip—this is *rug* burn."

Well shit.

That's not cool.

I laugh to myself, not stupid enough to say it out loud.

"You mean beard burn."

Teddy snorts. "Let's be honest, it's the exact same thing. I might as well have dragged my face and crotch across the carpet last night."

The visual almost makes me laugh.

"That wouldn't have been nearly as much fun." I grin, moving toward the coffee that's already brewed in the pot. Fill myself a mug, dump in a bunch of creamer, drop in some sugar, and lean against the counter, watching her.

Stir it with a spoon, sipping every so often as she regards me.

"It doesn't look terrible," I try, lying.

"Two minutes ago you asked why my face looked ruddy. *Ruddy*. Of *all* the words in the world to use."

"I mean…" It does though.

Dark red patches mar her otherwise beautiful skin like a rash, and I wonder what it looks like between her legs, on the insides of her silky thighs. Wonder if she'll let me have a look-see in the light of day.

"Could you not stare?"

"I can't help it." I laugh. "I've never done that to anyone before."

She scowls. "Yeah, because you're a freaking giant covered in hair. I cannot believe I made out with a guy they call Sasquatch. I mean, *really* Teddy?" She sounds appalled at herself.

"Technically, you didn't make out with anyone—I made out with your vagina."

She frowns harder. "You think you're funny, don't you?"

I smirk into my cup. "Maybe. I mean, it's not the end of the world."

"What am I going to say to my friends when they notice this?"

"Can't you cover it up with makeup?"

"Mariah is going to see me without it."

"So?"

"So! What am I going to say?"

"Tell her we made out and I went down on you." I shrug my shoulders. "What's the big deal?"

Her mouth opens. Closes. Opens again. "I…I can't…"

"It was oral, not anal. I don't see what the big deal is." Why is she acting so damn strange about this? "You can't tell your friends I went down on you?"

"No. I mean…yes. I mean no."

I stare, waiting for her to make some fucking sense.

"I can, I'm just not going to. They wouldn't understand."

Those chicks? The ones who get laid by someone different every weekend? They would applaud Teddy, not judge her for it.

My lips tighten into a straight line.

"If I said something about this—about us—they would keep asking for details, and then I would feel…*weird*, because we're not, you know…seeing each other or whatever."

I can see that happening. "I guess."

Teddy ducks her head again, hiding her face. Hiding her feelings and shit.

"Plus," she ventures slowly. "It's not like…" Clears her throat. "It's not going to happen again."

It's not?

Because I can still smell her on me—on the whiskers of my beard—and if she hadn't been sitting at the counter when I came up from the basement, I would have climbed back into bed with her, under the covers from the foot of the bed and woken her up between her legs.

Woken her tight ass up with my mouth on her delectable pussy.

Yeah.

I'm gonna want more of that.

"You can't un-ring a bell, Teddy Johnson."

"What?" My reference is clearly lost on her.

My wide shoulders shrug again. "You heard me. The deed is done—we can't go back so we might as well keep doing it."

"Um, I get we can't go back and undo it, but it doesn't mean we have to keep doing it. We should probably—"

"Too late."

"But—"

"Nope."

"Stop doing that."

"Next time you come over, I'll probably purposely cut the line for the furnace so it's freezing cold."

Teddy rolls her eyes and it's adorable. "Like I'd fall for that."

"Worth a try."

"What are you saying? That you want to have me over again?"

"Don't you like being here?"

"Yes, but I'm not going to come just so we can fool around."

"We'll watch movies too. And eat." Each other, obviously.

"Kip."

"*Teddy.*"

She stands, frustrated by the conversation. Grabs the jacket off the back of her chair and tosses her ponytail. "I should go."

I study her across the counter. "All right. Let me grab my keys and put shoes on."

She knows not to argue; we've had this conversation once before. Plus, it's colder than a witch's tit outside and I know she won't want to walk home. Not that I'd let her.

"Thank you."

Teddy watches as I squat, grab my boots, and tie the strings, one at a time, bent over at the waist, fingers at work. When I glance up, those brown eyes of hers are intense, fixated on my hands.

Yeah, that's right—these fingers were inside you last night. Take a long, hard look at them and imagine wanting them back on your body.

"I have a game tonight if you wanna come by." Pull my laces tight then get to work on the other boot.

"Tonight?" Her brows go up, surprised.

"Yeah. It's just a scrimmage, but it'll be fun—cold, but fun."

"Uh…maybe?"

"Teddy?"

"Hmm?"

"Don't overthink it, okay?"

"I'm not!" She answers too quickly, and I laugh, because she totally is.

"Sure you're not." I wink flirtatiously, rising to my full height. "You might like it—coming tonight, I mean."

I'm talking about the game, but it sounds like I mean something else.

"I'm sure I would."

"It's at Anderson Square Park. Five o'clock."

"All right."

"You'll come?"

"I'll…think about it."

She's going to come—I fucking know it. She's too sweet to stand me up.

Just like she's too nice to tell her "friend" to go fuck herself.

I make quick work of running her home, dropping her off in the front drive of her apartment building. Scowl when I think about the fact that she lives in a ground-level unit.

Remember that we still haven't exchanged numbers. "Want to put your cell in my phone?"

"Um, sure."

After, I let my car idle so I can watch her walk up to her building. She glances back over her shoulder twice, giving me a tentative little wave both times.

So damn cute.

***

TEDDY

Kip: *I have an assignment for you.*

Me: *Do I want to know what it is?*

Kip: *Probably not. And you'll probably think it's really inappropriate.*

Me: *Then maybe you shouldn't tell me.*

Kip: *Okay.*

Minutes tick by and I can't for the life of me conjure up a mature reply. Towel wrapped around my midsection, I lean against the counter, palming my phone, staring at the screen. Waiting for Kip to text me again.

He doesn't.

I can't stand it.

Me: *Fine. What is it?*

Kip: *You have to touch yourself inappropriately.*

Me: *What is that supposed to mean?*

Kip: *You know…masturbate.*

Me: *You're right—that's not at all an appropriate thing to say to someone.*

And he has completely shocked me.

Kip: *I thought we were past the stage of being awkward with each other.*

Me: *Nope. Definitely still at that stage.*

Kip: *Well shit…*

Kip: *You still going to come tonight or did I ruin it by being a pervert?*

Me: Don't worry. I'm still coming.

When I wipe the condensation off the mirror from the steam of my shower, I stand at the bathroom counter, staring at my reflection.

Consider my breasts. Shoulders.

Stomach.

The trimmed up patch of hair between my legs.

Feel myself blush, despite the flush from the hot shower I just took, chest and neck growing redder with each second I stand here, watching myself.

I can't do it.

I cannot touch myself.

Well, I can, just not like that.

Except…I rise to my tiptoes and spread my legs a little, bending my head down to survey the damage Kip's beard caused.

Red, red, red.

Red between my thighs, just like I knew it would be.

Sore too.

Why am I sore? I didn't have sex.

Is this normal?

Should I google it? What would I even search: sore after receiving oral sex? Why are my legs so sore after a guy has gone down on me? Why do my inner thighs have slight bruising?

My face gets hot thinking about it.

Thinking about him.

The change in him, overnight, talking to me like he

wants…more. He hasn't said it, but he's not looking at me the same way. He looks at me like…he's developing a crush on me. This morning, in his kitchen, when he looked me up and down, I swear he wanted to haul me up and carry me back upstairs and…do stuff.

It took everything I had not to look at the crotch of his pants to check for a boner.

The whole thing is so unsettling for me. I'm not used to male attention, not used to someone like him wanting me as something other than a friend.

The whole thing has my stomach in knots.

My hand goes there, resting on my belly. Presses down so I can even out my breathing.

Is this what it feels like to have butterflies?

Should he be the one giving them to me? This isn't what I planned for myself—he is not my type, not even *close*. When I picture myself with a guy, I imagine him clean-cut. Handsome. No facial hair, certainly not some-one with hair prettier than mine.

Kip vaguely reminds me of that Brock guy, the Insta-Famous dude who makes videos of himself throwing his hair up into a bun—but hairier. And less cocky and full of himself.

Kissing him with the beard wasn't as bad as I'd thought it would be—had I thought about it. Sure, it could prob-ably use some conditioning to make it softer, but all in all, not the worst.

If you don't count the rash on my cheeks.

My phone chimes and I pick it up, expecting Kip, heart racing.

Instead, I'm disappointed to see it's from a guy in one of my civil law classes, hounding me about the banquet the engineering department has coming up—an event I cannot afford to attend, let alone contribute to in the way of a donation.

I wouldn't even be going if it weren't for this grant—they're presenting it to me there, but I still have to buy a ticket.

How stupid is that?

Tyler: Hey. We're trying to get a final headcount for the fundraiser. You getting a ticket or what?

Me: I still don't know why I have to buy a ticket when I'm there to receive a grant...LAME

Tyler: Because it's a FUNDRAISER, Theodora. The department needs money too.

I don't know how Tyler found out my real name, but he uses it frequently and it drives me nuts. Like we're friends and he has the privilege.

Me: I know, I know, I'm just really broke right now. I don't really have the extra money for a ticket, that's all.

Tyler: You want me to put you down for a donation then if you don't plan to be there for the dinner? We're putting together baskets for the silent auction.

I just said I didn't have any money! Why would I want to give them a donation? Ugh! He's asked me about this no less than ten times and I've said no each and every one.

Me: I don't think so. NO to the donation. Do not put me down for one. Haha.

Tyler: But yes for the dinner?

Me: It's not like I have a choice, do I? I'll look like an asshole if I stand in back of the room while everyone else is eating LOL

Tyler: *One ticket or two?*

I want to bang my head against a desk.

Me: *How much are the tickets? Remind me.*

Tyler: *$25 for a single, $35 for a couple*

Me: *Umm... Hmm...*

I chew on my lower lip; if I buy a couple's ticket, I could bring someone. A date.

Kip springs to mind.

Do I have the lady balls to ask him to be my date for something as important as *this*? What would I say? If I ask him, would he get the wrong idea about it?

I'm pretty sure most of my friends from the department will be bringing dates, and I'd feel less self-conscious if I brought one too.

But Kip?

He's not really a safe choice; what if he says something off-color and embarrasses me? What if he's eating and ends up with food in his beard and makes it awkward?

I've never seen him in any other setting besides a rugby party and his house.

I'm getting way ahead of myself here, but Tyler keeps blowing up my phone, and I should make a decision.

Me: *I guess I'll do a couple's ticket.*

Tyler: *Cool.*

His reply annoys me, and I turn my phone over on the counter and resume blow-drying my hair. I'll think about what to do later—maybe the mood will strike me to ask him after his rugby match today.

I face the mirror, brushing the wet strands aside, and look myself in the eye.

"Kip, would you like to attend a banquet with me?" I ask my reflection. "Just as friends. It wouldn't be an actual date." I run a brush through my hair. "Kip, wanna come to a thing with me? No biggie if you can't. Whatever."

I sigh. I suck so hard at this.

"Hey Kip, great game—uh, match. So, I was wondering, if you're not doing anything next Friday, I have this thing I have to be at..."

For some reason, the brush is at my mouth like a microphone, like I'm reporter at the scene of a story. I cringe and set it on the counter.

Maybe I should text him this week. It would certainly be easier. If I wait long enough, he'll make plans for Friday, and say no, then I'm off the hook.

But if I do and he says no, it will be on my phone, in writing, for all eternity, and I'll have to see it every time he texts me.

He won't say no, a little voice inside me says.

Who am I kidding—he's going to say yes.

He'll say yes, because I have terrible luck, and then I'll actually have to take the Neanderthal out in public; no doubt he'll wear those god awful work boots.

We'll have fun, though.

Me and Sasquatch.

I groan, smile into the mirror, and hum.

SECOND SATURDAY (AT GAME)

"The day I just sit here and watch them throw their balls around."

TEDDY

I'm not the only girl here flying solo, but I'm the only one here without a blanket or a chair.

Why didn't I think to bring one?

I scan the area, searching for a dry spot.

Lower myself to the ground, sitting cross-legged, facing the rugby field. Comb the bodies for Kip, watching for his familiar form among the giants.

I know they're not all as large as he is, but from this vantage point, they're all Goliaths. Hairy legs, high sport socks already stained with mud and grass and matching jerseys. Far too many broad chests to count.

And then…

There he is.

Stretching, torso bent, his thick thighs and ass are

thrust in my direction. Even in the cluster of broody man children, he stands apart with his air of conceit as he moves to get limber.

Kip has that mop of hair pulled up, twisted at the top of his head, and is wearing a headband—along with a rubber band in his beard too, and that makes my lips curl at the corner.

What the hell is that all about?

I continue to study him.

The mouth guard he's just popped into place over his teeth. The bright blue cleats digging into the ground. The band around his bicep with the letter C on it.

I didn't know he was the captain of the team—then again, I've never really asked him about it.

"Who are you here to see?" a voice asks from behind me, startling me out of my scrutiny.

I twist around.

Two girls stand with plaid Iowa blankets in their arms, staring down at me curiously.

"We've never seen you here before," one of them says. She has brunette hair and a pleasant smile, and in her right hand she's clutching a coffee cup. "But figured since you were here alone, you must be dating one of the guys and not just jock-chasing."

I blush despite the cold. "Oh, um, I'm a friend of Kip Carmichael. He, uh, invited me."

"Kip Carmichael…invited you." It's more of a statement than a question, and four eyebrows shoot up.

I hurry to explain. "We're friends."

"Friends. Whatever you sayyyy…" the one with black

hair sing-songs. "Mind if we sit? We can tell you all the rules of the game."

I groan.

More rules.

"I'm Renee," the brunette says. "And this is Miranda. I'm dating Brian Freeman—he's number four." She points a purple fingernail toward the field. "And Miranda is engaged to number thirteen, Thomas Dennison."

Engaged? *Whoa.*

Miranda thrusts out her hand, displaying the tiny rock on her left ring finger. "Only four hundred and ninety-seven more days!" she squeals, spreading out her blanket and taking a seat next to me. "Want to share? The ground is so cold. Did you think there would be bleachers?"

I did. "Kind of?"

"Usually there are, but this is just a scrimmage, so they're not playing on an actual field. This is more, like, for fun."

"More like an exhibition game," Renee clarifies.

Miranda moves her hand this way and that, admiring her engagement ring. "We always have to sit here and hope they don't get hurt during one of these games."

"What happens if they get hurt?"

"Wellll," Miranda begins. "For one, they can't play—*obviously*—and two, a few of these guys want to play overseas. You know, in Britain or wherever."

"It's really popular in England," Renee explains. "More so than here. No one gives a crap about it here."

"Do your boyfriends want to play after college?"

Miranda takes a chug of whatever is in her coffee cup. "Thomas doesn't, even though I'd like him to 'cause—hello! England—I would love to live there even if Thomas doesn't. But I think that twat Steven plans to at least try. And number two—he's really good."

Twat.

I've never in my life heard a female call someone that before.

"I bet Kip could if he wanted to. He's good, plus he's like, gi*nor*mous. The professional players are all super huge."

Super huge.

Yeah, he is.

Tall. Broad. *Big.*

Everywhere.

I try my best not to think about his dick, but it's impossible—especially considering he's one hundred feet in front of me, wearing spandex compression shorts, the outline of his jock strap leaving nothing to the imagination.

As if he knows we're watching, he adjusts himself, squatting for a few seconds and shifts his cock inside the cup before resuming his stretches.

Yup. His dick is *big* all right, just like the rest of him, and I dry humped it nice and good last night before he went down on me.

My sore thighs are proof of that.

"So you're friends with Kip, eh? He never has people come to the games." Miranda watches him with me, fiddling with the rim of her cup. "Although one time, I think he had a sister that showed up, because they left together after."

"How do you know it was his sister?" Renee wants to know.

"She was tall. Plus, same hair." Miranda laughs. "God, isn't it just awful? If Thomas grew his out like that, I'd break up with him." She gives her dark hair a toss, sets down her cup, and adjusts the scarf wrapped around her pretty neck. "I wonder what it would be like to sleep with a guy who had hair longer than mine."

"Uh—weird?" Renee says. "So gross. Like, cut it."

I wouldn't say it was weird; I'd say it was different—not that we had sex or anything, but we did sleep together, and he did have it pulled up. It wasn't lying loose around his shoulders, and, come to think of it, have I ever really seen it down?

Maybe just while he was redoing his man bun.

Miranda stares at Kip again, thinking. "I remember Molly—our friend who used to date one of these guys—said Kip didn't always have the beard and was kind of hot."

"Well he isn't hot now." Renee laughs. "No offense."

I realize then I haven't told her my name. "Oh my gosh, duh—I'm Teddy."

"Teddy? I love that!" Renee cries. "It's so cool!"

"Oh my god, me too!" Miranda gushes. "Don't you just love male names for women? They're my favorite. In fact, when Thomas and I have babies—I'm having like, ten kids—my girls are going to have boy names. Frankie, Georgie, Max…"

"Teddy?" I throw out.

"Oh I'm *def* adding that to the short list." She picks up

her cup again. "You want a sip? It's hot chocolate."

"No thanks."

I can't believe how friendly these girls are. They're nothing like Cameron and Tessa, and they're definitely friendlier than Mariah, who would never have befriended a stranger at a sporting event—unless it was a guy.

"I don't think I've ever seen you at the rugby house before," I venture cautiously.

Renee makes a face. "That's because we don't hang out there. It's nothing but cleat chasers and gold diggers— I won't let Brian party there without me anymore."

"Right," Miranda agrees. "Besides, the house is so dirty. No one cleans it."

"What about you?" Renee asks. "Do you hang out there?"

I laugh. "Ugh, that's where I met Kip. He, um, caught me at the keg, pouring beer for people, and—I don't know. We became friends in an awkward sort of way."

"Awkward sort of way? What do you mean?" Miranda cocks her head, interested.

"You know, we've been hanging out at his place, and just…it's different. He doesn't give a shit about what anyone thinks, and he's kind of rude, and sometimes I'm shy so we're opposites that way. Plus, I didn't think I'd like him because of the whole beard thing. It was really off-putting at first, but…he's grown on me."

Grown on me—an understatement if there ever was one.

"And you're *just* friends?"

"I mean…yes?"

"Why the question mark at the end?" Renee leans in. "Do you like him?"

"I might?"

"Does he like you?"

He likes my body, I can't stop myself from thinking.

"Shit—he sees you! Act natural." Miranda nudges me in the ribcage. "Don't look at him!"

I look.

She clocks me again. "I said don't look at him."

"Why? Why can't I look?"

"Guy 101, that's why! If he sees you watching, he's going to think you don't have a life and you just came here to see him."

That makes no sense.

None.

At all.

"But I am watching. That is exactly why I'm here—to see him." I sound like I'm defending myself, but there's laughter in my voice.

I'm having fun with these two—more fun than I've had with Mariah in a long, long time.

"Miranda, give her a break." Renee giggles. "Okay, he's not looking over here anymore. You can relax."

Like that's going to happen. "Can I watch him once the game starts?"

"It's called a match, and yes, you can watch him once it starts, which is in"—she checks her phone—"less than ten minutes. They usually try to start on time."

"I hope they call it early—I'm *freez*ing, and Thomas is taking me to dinner."

"Speaking of freezing," I carefully start. "I was, um, at Kip's last night, and he had no heat. It was awful."

I'm desperate to discuss what happened with someone who isn't going to have an angle, like Mariah, who would pump me for information about Kip—not for me, but for herself.

I've realized over the past few weekends that she doesn't have my best interests at heart, not like a best friend should, and it's probably time to distance myself from her.

"You were at Kip's place, and you had no heat. Interestinggggggg." Miranda wiggles her eyebrows. "So what did you do to keep warm?"

More brow wiggles.

"We..." I hesitate. I've never engaged in girl talk like this before, gossiping about my own relationships, because I've never had any to gossip about. I test the waters. "Snuggled."

"You snuggled." Neither of them look impressed with my answer.

I nod, biting down on my lower lip before busting out into a smile.

"Did this snuggling include any exchange of bodily fluid?" Miranda impishly smirks over the rim of her cup.

"Miranda! That's private!" Renee scolds her. Then she turns to me. "But did it?"

I'm not sure what they mean by that exactly, but, "Some, I guess?"

"Did you do it?" Miranda has no filter. Or boundaries.

"No! Nothing like that."

"Oh." She's clearly disappointed.

"But he did go down…" I point to my vajayjay. "There."

"Stop it right now! He went down on you? What was it like with, you know—the beard?"

Ha! I knew girls were obsessed with beards and oral.

"Let me just put it to you this way: I'm walking crooked and I have rug burn on the insides of my thighs." I lean back, bracing myself with both palms on the blanket, feeling smug at having impressed these girls.

"Oh. My. God! Did you orgasm more than once?" Miranda hovers in my personal space.

I sit up. "You can do that?"

"Are you being serious right now? Yes, you can have more than one gasm. One time, Thomas gave me three—two from eating me out, and then he fucked me from behind. My god, I was exhausted."

"Miranda!" Renee is horrified. "What the hell? Too much information!"

Miranda rolls her eyes. "Puh-lease, I told you all this already."

"But we just met Teddy, like, five minutes ago," Renee chastises. "Give her a minute to get to know us before you scare her away. Ease into it, Jesus!"

"Teddy isn't going anywhere, are you Teddy?" She pats me on the shoulder. "She's going to be one of us, I can tell." Miranda winks flirtatiously.

"I didn't say we were dating, you guys," I hasten to point out. "I might not come back."

"Not yet, but Kip has looked over at you at least a dozen times in the last three minutes, so I'd say you were headed that way, especially if he asked you to be here in the first place. And went down on you last night."

"Did you give him a blowjob?" Renee blurts out, and has Miranda letting out a peal of laughter.

"You just yelled at me for getting too personal, you hypocrite."

Renee covers her mouth with her hands, laughing. "I'm sorry, it just came out. Teddy, you don't have to answer that."

"Yes she does," Miranda chides. "Kidding, only if you want to."

"I...didn't. Should I have?"

"Did he want you to?"

"He didn't say."

"He didn't ask for a blowie?" Miranda's brows are in her hairline. "Dang girl—you've got yourself a unicorn."

"What do you mean?"

"He gave you oral without wanting it in return? That's a true find, my friend. Thomas always wants a BJ after he's gone down on me, unless I let him bang me."

"Um, I didn't let him, uh...bang me, but...we did dry hump first. Does that count?"

"You dry fucked first? That is so hot."

"I remember when Brian and I used to dry hump all the time." Renee recalls it wistfully, gazing off into the line of trees at the back of the park. "I'm *totally* doing that to him tonight. I'm gonna try to make him come in his boxers for old time's sake."

"Like when we were in high school—I was always afraid to get pregnant, so I would only let my boyfriend dry fuck me through my clothes. God, I was such a prude."

"It's not prudish—it's sexy."

"Right, but do you know how much chafing is involved? *Dude.* So much chafing."

These girls are too much.

I lie back on the blanket, laughing up at the sky, and they join me until we hear a whistle blowing, three short blasts.

"Op! Match is starting." I get a pat on the thigh. "Pay attention, and we'll talk you through it so you know what's going on. It looks like football but the rules are completely different."

"It's mostly guys who like to pile on top of each other, get dirty, punch each other in the face, and then go drinking afterward," Renee teases.

For once, Miranda is the serious one. "Stop that—you know that's not true. Rugby is a real physical strain on their bodies. See? They've only been playing thirty seconds and that guy is already limping."

"That guy is a *pussy*," Renee mumbles under her breath about the opposing player limping to the sideline. He's replaced quickly by another giant. "And those pileups are called scrums. It's part of the game."

I nod, though I don't understand.

Some of the guys are wearing helmets; most of them aren't. They're all wearing mouth guards, their jerseys all stained. Each and every one of them has bruises, gashes, and scrapes.

I hadn't noticed them on Kip before, but I'm noticing them now. The dark bruise on his thigh I didn't see in the dark. A cut on his forehead, right at his hairline.

"How long do these things last?" I ask.

"Eighty minutes. Two halves."

"Basically an eternity, unless they're playing someone really good, like Penn State or Notre Dame."

Notre Dame.

"Oo! Watch, watch, watch—Thomas is about to get pummeled. Ugh, why does he do shit like that?"

"Do shit like what?" I ask. "What did he do?"

"He always has to be in the middle of those stupid scrums—he's going to get hurt again."

The players from both teams are huddled in the middle of the field, and it looks like a giant bar fight as each man struggles to gain control of the ball.

"Who invented this? It looks awful." My voice sounds dazed as I watch men jump on top of each other, throwing elbows, shoulders, and gabs. "Jesus, where are the refs?"

"Right? Brian spends the whole next day after one of these complaining, icing himself, and bandaging up bloody wounds." She smiles. "I think he feels really masculine playing this stupid game, like a gladiator or something."

I can see that—no padding, no hard helmets, nothing to prevent them from getting seriously injured.

Spandex shorts.

Perfect asses and toned backs. Thick thighs. Muscular arms.

It's hard not to stare, hard not to appreciate how hard

and fine these bodies are.

They're rough. They're dirty.

Some of them are as hairy as Kip, but not many.

I train my eyes on him as he dips low to tackle an opponent, heels digging into the ground for traction.

"What position is he? Fullback? Linebacker?"

"You're confusing rugby with soccer and football." Miranda chuckles. "Kip is a loose head because he's bigger and heavier. They wouldn't put him in the back—they need him in the front."

"Not that he stays there." Renee smirks. "He's a ball hog."

That doesn't surprise me.

"So what's his job?"

"Well…hmm." Miranda thinks. "He lifts guys up in the scrum—that giant pile we just saw. He mauls people like a savage and shoves dudes out of the way."

Renee nods along her agreement. "Yup. That about sums it up, but if you really want to find out more, google it."

I will. For sure.

The game drags on, the ground unrelentingly cold. I'm relieved when the final whistle blows and the referee calls the game in our favor. The girls pack up to leave, and I rise along with them since I brought *nothing*.

"Come over with us and say hi to Kip." Renee has the blanket folded over her arm and pulls at my jacket with her free hand.

"No, that's okay. You guys go, I'm gonna just…I'm

gonna go."

"Why? He'll be happy to see you."

"I…no. I'll feel weird. We're not dating or anything."

Rushing the boys after the match seems like a girl-friend-y thing to do, and I know I'm not close to that level with Kip.

"You sure?"

"Yeah, I'm sure." He's not likely to notice when I don't show up at their side.

The two girls rush off to gush over their boyfriends and congratulate them on their victory, hugging and kissing them all over. I give Kip one last look before turning my back—he's bent over the bench, untying a cleat, perfect rear end in the air, black socks highlighting his ridiculous calves.

I sigh, walking toward the car I borrowed from Tessa to get here, the beige Camry she's been sweet enough to loan me from time to time to make my life easier.

It'll be a few more years before I'll be able to save enough to afford a car.

"Teddy! Wait up."

I pause at Kip's voice, at the sound of his cleats click-ing across the pavement in my direction.

"Where you goin'?"

I look him up and down.

"How are you so dirty?" are the first words out of my mouth by way of greeting, because honestly, he's filthy. Positively covered in dirt and grime. "It's not even *rain-ing*—how are you caked with mud?"

Those giant shoulders shrug. "Don't know."

He looks like a Viking warrior, tall and imposing and blond. Beard knotted with that rubber band, so it's out of his way, hair falling out all over the damn place.

He's a Viking who just did battle in a yellow and black jersey.

Feet spread apart, he's breathing heavily and regarding me under the now illuminated street lamps. We've been here so long it's gotten dark, the parking lot beginning to empty as players and spectators head home.

"So...where you going?" he asks again, hands going up behind his head. Biceps bulging.

"Home?"

"Why?"

Uh. Was home not the right answer? "I have to return Tessa's car, but, I mean, I don't have plans to do anything."

"You're not coming over?"

He wants me to come over? He saw me last night and this morning—isn't that enough? "I didn't know you want-ed me to."

"I don't have any plans either."

"Of course not—it's not Friday night." I find myself winking at him flirtatiously.

"We could go see a movie." His legs are still spread apart, the cold air causing his breath—and mine—to puff out in a slow stream of steam.

"After the match you just played? You must be tired." And beat, if the blood on his jersey is any indication, the scratch on his knee and the gash in his lip...

Jesus, he looks like hell.

Like a total brute.

And I kind of like it.

"Or we could order a pizza, ice my leg, and sit around doing nothing," he offers, hands still clasped behind his head. It makes his chest look wider and harder, mesh jersey stretched taught across it.

Damn he's in good shape.

"That's what I usually do," he goes on.

"We could."

His arms come down, hands falling to his sides, settling the matter. "I'll follow you so you can drop off Tessa's car then take you to my place."

He says it casually, as if it's that easy, like we've done it a million times before.

"All right."

"Cool."

Cool.

SECOND SATURDAY (AFTER GAME)

"Go ahead. Touch it."

KIP

Something is on Teddy's mind; I can tell by the way she keeps looking at me. Small, quick, furtive glances when she thinks I'm not watching her—which I am.

She's been flushed since we got to my place, a ball of nervous energy I can't quite figure out the cause of.

It's not like she hasn't been here before.

It's not like I haven't touched her tits or had my tongue in her pussy.

I plop an ice pack on my swollen knee at the same time my eyes drop to her breasts. Her flat stomach. Legs tucked neatly under her ass as she sits beside me on the living room floor.

She moves just then, uncurling herself and stretching out, wiggling her toes when she extends them out in front of her. The nails are painted a pretty bright pink.

"Nice toes."

She wiggles them again. "Thanks."

Nice toes. Nice tits. Nice...everything.

It's a damn shame it was dark when I went down on her last night; I'm dying to see her naked, dying to see her spread out on my bed again. I want to hear her moan and feel her grabbing at my hair.

We plowed through an entire large pizza over two hours ago, and neither of us are watching the movie we selected, some comedy about some old guys who play tag *blah blah blah who gives a shit.*

"Should we watch something else?" I offer, bored.

"Nah. It's getting late."

It is.

I flip my phone to check the time: 12:29.

"I should get going," Teddy says hesitantly, fiddling with the hem on her basic, gray T-shirt.

"Or...you could spend the night." I throw her a lazy smile. "Heat's fixed." Meaning: neither of us will freeze if we get naked.

She pauses. "It is fixed, isn't it?"

"Yup. Did it all by myself, remember?"

"So handy," she teases. "On a scale of one to ten, how sore are you?"

I consider the question. "Five."

Fifteen, but I don't tell her that. I don't want her being gentle with me in case she decides to stay and get handsy with me later.

"Only five?" Doubt is written all over her gorgeous

face. "Why don't I believe you?"

"Because I'm an accomplished liar. Plus, the beard hides most of my expression." I grin wolfishly.

"You don't think I should leave?"

"Only if you want to." I give her toes a tap with my big toe.

"What do you want me to do?"

Oh shit—she's going to make me say it. Why do girls do this? Doesn't she get that by me saying *You could spend the night*, I'm telling her I want her to spend the night? She needs me to spell it out for her, now, too?

Ugh. Fuck me. "I want you to stay." *And I don't want you sleeping in the guest bedroom. I want you sleeping with me. Under me. Over me. Sideways.*

"Do you want to spoon me too?"

I want to do more than spoon her.

I realize Teddy is a virgin, but that doesn't stop me from wanting her.

She's amazing company. She's sweet, pretty, and smart. She has a kind heart and a great ass, and who can beat all that?

"Yup."

"I don't have pajamas."

Pretty sure my nostrils flare just then. The fact that she doesn't have anything to sleep in gets me excited.

I grin. "Me either."

"Are you even tired?"

What does that have to do with bedtime? "Actually, yes."

Though now I wish like hell that I wasn't.

"Me too."

I rise then offer my hand to help her up. Plant a kiss on the crown of her head, and...take her fucking hand.

Jesus.

So domestic.

I let her lead the way up the stairs, gaze resting on her tight ass and the sway of her hips.

We make quick work of brushing our teeth; Teddy washes her face, uses the toilet.

Then, when we're standing next to the bed and she's fully clothed, it's suddenly so fucking awkward and the only thing to do is help her out of them. Because I'm a gentleman, and that's what we fucking do.

The T-shirt comes first.

I lift it over her head, letting it drop to the floor. "Is this okay?"

"Yes," she whispers.

The lights are on, so I can see every inch of her skin. Her high breasts in the white cotton bra she's got on. Nothing lace, nothing too sexy. Just Teddy.

I leave the bra, and together we go for the waistband of her black leggings.

Push them down, over her hips until she's able to step out of them.

Practical, white cotton panties.

No thong. No hip-huggers. No flirty cheeksters.

Sweet.

Sensible.

She turns and hops up into bed. Crawls to the center and burrows beneath the covers. Yanks them clear up to her chin, only her shoulders and bra straps visible.

It makes me want to tunnel under the blankets and do dirty, nasty shit to her.

I leave the bedside lamp on.

Climb in.

Lie flat on my back, arms behind my head, staring at the ceiling.

"Thanks for coming today." *And later.*

"Thanks for inviting me. It was an education, that's for sure."

I roll over to face her. "Did you have fun?"

"Yeah—I met Renee and Miranda."

Who? "Who are they?"

"Um, Brian's and Thomas's girlfriends."

"Oh, those two. Yeah, they're decent. I see them around a lot. They come to almost every game, even the away ones."

"Really?"

"Yeah."

"Well they were super helpful, telling me the rules—I didn't know how the game was played."

"But it was fun?"

"It was. Lots of blood, though, which I thought was weird."

I laugh, chuckling deep in my chest. "That's what I

love about it."

Teddy rolls her eyes, shifting onto her side to face me and mimicking my pose.

We're inches apart now, her cleavage a thing of beauty, plump and right there in my fucking face. I want to trail a finger between her boobs but don't have the guts.

Instead, Teddy surprises me by trailing a finger between mine—my pecs—running the tip down my flat stomach on a clear path to my happy trail.

It makes my dick twitch.

I give her a lazy smile and let her touch me.

It's killing me to lie here, unflinching, just observing her.

"You…" she begins shyly. "You're beautiful."

"So are you."

Teddy ducks her head, blushing down into the valley of her tits. "No I'm not."

"Yes you are." I reach for her then, hand on her waist beneath the covers. "You're gorgeous."

I would never say that to someone unless I meant it.

"I can't believe I'm lying here not wearing any clothes." She laughs nervously. "This is so unlike me."

"Is it?"

"Yes."

"Do you want to put your clothes back on?"

Another laugh. "No."

Good.

"I want…" Teddy clears her throat. "I want you to kiss

me."

So I do.

We gravitate toward one another, our lips softly meeting, and I'm conscious of the fact that my fucking mustache is partially preventing me from feeling her mouth.

I trimmed my beard back this afternoon, but it's still too long, making it impossible for Teddy to stroke the skin on my jaw, my chin, my neck.

Robs me of the sensitive spots I used to love having sucked and nipped by delicate lips.

Our mouths open and fuse, tongues touching—tentatively at first then hungrily as the erection grows in my boxers.

"Are you going to dry hump me again?" She grins.

"Do you want me to?"

"I don't know, but I don't think I'm ready to have sex with you."

"You don't have to have sex with me—that's not why I wanted you to spend the night. I just wanted to spend the *night* with you. That's all."

Because maybe I'm finally sick of being alone all the damn time.

Maybe it's time to let someone else in, someone I didn't know I needed until I met Teddy.

Funny how the universe works, isn't it? Shit drops on you when you're staring at the sky, wondering what to do with your life, and sometimes it's just what you fucking need, right when you need it.

Teddy is that something I needed.

"I think I want to…" Her voice cuts off. "I don't know how to even say this. It's so embarrassing."

"What? You can tell me."

"I've never given a blowjob before."

Excuse me, say what now? "I'm all ears."

The laugh erupting from her belly has butterflies dancing in mine.

"Would you knock it off? I'm nervous. I mean, I want to, I just don't know how."

"Uh…everyone knows how." *You put it in your mouth—preferably the entire thing—and suck.* Obviously I don't say that out loud—I don't want her to think I'm a complete douchebag—but how hard can blowing a guy be? "I don't think there is such a thing as a bad blowjob, unless you bite down on it."

"What!"

"I don't think there is such a thing as a bad—"

"No, I heard you just fine. I just can't believe you said it. Have you ever heard of a guy getting his…you know… bitten?"

"No. Thank God." *Jesus Christ.* I don't want to picture anyone's teeth biting my dick and never should have said anything. The visual makes me shudder. "No to teeth."

"But what if it doesn't *fit* properly—like it's too big and I can't help but scrape it with my teeth?"

"Guess we'll have to see, won't we?"

That makes her blush good and hard, and now I'm good and hard, cock throbbing with anticipation.

I wait for her to move first, lying still, not wanting to

spook her.

Seconds pass before she makes up her mind to go for it, peeling back the blanket covering my waist. Peers at my boner, tentatively studying it before going in for the kill.

Fingertip dragging along the elastic of my boxer briefs.

Dragging them down *jussttt* far enough to expose the tip of my cock. Brushes it with her thumb, circling the little hole at the top.

Oh Jesus, she's going to slowly kill me.

"I think this might be my favorite part."

"Which part?"

"This." The pad of her forefingers buffs the tip, spreading the clear liquid that's appeared. "The head. It's...sexy."

Uh huh.

"Sometimes, when I'm lying in bed at night, I watch small clips of porn, know what I mean?" Her finger teases me. "And once I saw this couple *doing it*, and he never put it all the way in."

Oh my god.

"I think I want to do that."

Yeah—we're totally fucking doing that. We're going to play a little game of *just the tip*.

"It looks like it feels good."

Fuck yeah it would feel good.

Teddy looks at my face, and I realize I haven't uttered a single goddamn word since she started touching my cock.

"Does this feel okay? You look..."

"Yes." My breath hitches when she connects her thumb

and forefinger, cuffing the head of my dick. Leisurely moves up and down.

"I could do this all night," she muses lazily.

Please don't—I will die if you do. The ripples of pleasure from that singular, tiny motion would surely slowly kill me.

My boxers get pushed down farther, and I lift my hips so she can slide them all the way down. Kick them off when they hit my ankles, send them flying toward *who gives a shit.*

After that, Teddy doesn't talk, only making sounds from the back of her throat. Sounds like appreciation and pleasure—the same ones I'm making, because I have no self-control left.

Both my hands clutch at the pillow under my head, fisting it while Teddy plays with my cock and balls, and I'm so hard I want to come *now.*

It won't take me long when—if—she finally puts me in her mouth. It'll be the world's shortest blowjob, done and over within minutes, I fucking know it.

My hips buck when she licks it, testing the feel of it on her tongue. I blow out a puff of pent-up breath, my lungs contracting more rapidly by the second.

It sounds like I can't catch my breath.

I sound like I'm...

About to beg her to, "Suck it. God, *please* put it in your mouth. *Please.*"

New to the game but still a woman with wiles, Teddy cocks an eyebrow, an air of triumph on her face. She knows she is in control and she likes it.

"You want me to suck it?"

"Yes."

"You want me to…put this in my mouth?" She licks it again.

My mouth forms the word *yes*, but no sounds actually leave my lips.

My balls throb.

My chest burns.

And when she takes my dick and puts it between her lips, my entire body clenches from the pleasure of it.

Jesus, it's been so long since anyone has blown me, I'd almost forgotten how good it feels. How much I enjoy the sight of a woman's head down by my pelvis and the view of just the top of her head as she bobs it up and down.

My fingers grip the pillow tighter so I don't reach for Teddy's hair, yank it a little like I want to—that might scare the shit out of her—or push her head down so I impale her mouth.

Mouth.

Hand.

Lips. Tongue.

All of them working together, and *goddamn if it isn't perfect.*

***

"Kip?"

"Hmm?" I trace her belly button with my forefinger, round and round and round. The same belly button I licked with my tongue an hour ago before spreading her legs and eating her out.

Mmm mmm good. My new favorite meal.

"There was something I wanted to ask you—feel free to say no."

"That's not exactly a ringing endorsement of this *something*, is it?"

"Sorry. I'm not good at asking people for favors."

Favors.

I brace myself, waiting for her to want what all the girls before her wanted: Kip, babe, can I borrow some cash? Kip, can you get us tickets to a concert? Kip, can we go to St. Bart's for spring break and stay at your parents' beach house?

My "What?" comes out clipped and shorter than I planned—but damn, I wish she'd just spit the request out already so I can say *no*, shove her out of my bed, and never see her again.

"I have this dinner—a banquet next weekend, and, um…I'm receiving that grant I was telling you about?"

The stiff muscles in my body relax a fraction. "Yeah?"

"I was wondering if you wanted to come with me." Teddy clears her throat. "I bought two tickets."

She bought two tickets.

I twist my torso, pulling her in. Relief flooding my body. "You want me to be your date for a banquet?"

"It's a fundraiser for the engineering department, but… I mean, yes—only if you're not doing anything Saturday night."

I do have a match that day, but it's early, and I'd have plenty of time to take her to a banquet.

"I'm free Saturday night."

"So you can go?"

"I can go." In fact, I'd *love* to.

***

Me: *So I kind of have a problem.*

Ronnie: *I KNEW IT! I knew you had a small penis— I've told everyone and they never believe me 'cause you're so tall.*

Me: *Would you be serious for one second?*

Ronnie: *Oh crap—you're being serious? Well shit. Okay—go. What do you need?*

Me: *Remember Teddy?*

Ronnie: *Obviously. I've even been creeping on her on social media. You're welcome, by the way, for my superior stalking skills*

Me: *FOR WHAT??*

Ronnie: *I had to make sure she was normal—I also looked up her court records too, just in case things with the two of you took a turn for the best.*

Me: *You are unbelievable.*

Ronnie: *So did they? Take a turn for the best, or the worst?*

Me: *She asked me to a thing. A benefit.*

Ronnie: *A benefit??? Ugh, SOCIAL CLIMBER. I freaking KNEW IT!!!!! Run. RUN KIPLING!*

Me: *Knock it off, it's not that kind of benefit. It's for the engineering department, she's receiving a grant.*

Ronnie: *Oh. Well, don't I feel foolish **awkward*

laugh** You were saying?

Me: *My question is, what do I do? Do I buy a suit or what? It's on campus, so it's not formal, but I still think I should look nice, but I don't have anything dressy with me here.*

Ronnie: *Do you at least have a polo shirt or something?*

Me: *Yeah, I think so.*

Ronnie: *There's your answer then. Wear that, trim that beard up, and do something with your hair, and you won't have to go buy anything.*

Me: *You think I should shave?*

Ronnie: *Uhhhh, I mean...only if you want to. You only just met the girl, and it's taken you two years to grow that monstrosity. BUT...*

Me: *But?*

Ronnie: *It would be a huge gesture. If you like her.*

Me: *So I should shave, and wear a polo shirt, and not worry about a suit.*

Ronnie: *Right.*

Me: *Okay. I can manage that.*

Ronnie: *Wait—you're seriously going to shave??? Holy shit.*

Ronnie: *You LIKE THIS GIRL?????? For real. No bullshitting.*

Me: *Have you been listening to a thing I said?*

Ronnie: *You have said NOTHING. You've had her over TWICE and you've hung out on Fridays and THAT IS ALL YOU'VE GIVEN ME. You throw NO BONES.*

Me: Yes, I fucking like her.

Ronnie: Mom is going to freak. You know that, right?

Me: Mom isn't going to find out yet, VERONICA.

Ronnie: Fine…but when it's time to tell her, I get to leak the information. Deal?

Me: Deal.

THIRD SATURDAY

"She cleans up nice and makes me want to bang her."

TEDDY

"What's with the dress?" Mariah is leaned against the door to the bathroom, studying my reflection in the mirror as I apply another coat of mascara.

Makeup I'd asked her to help me with an hour ago.

She said she was too busy, yet here she is, standing there in yoga pants, hair tossed up into a messy top knot, clearly not doing anything productive.

She could have helped me.

"I have that banquet tonight. The one where I'm receiving my grant."

"A scholarship thing?" I can see her eyes roaming up and down my back. "It looks like you have date."

I draw in a breath, not sure how much I want to tell her about Kip, or how she'll react. She knows nothing; not since the night she whispered in his ear and propositioned him.

He still hasn't told me what she said, but what else

could it possibly have been?

"It's a bit of both, I guess?"

"Are you going with someone?" She's interested now, studying her nails in that way she does when she's pretending not to care. Feigning disinterest when she's insatiably curious.

It's such a bitchy thing to do.

Why can't she be happy for me?

"Yes. I'm going with someone." I purposely omit details, knowing it's going to drive her crazy not knowing who my date it.

One of her hand flops over, wrist holding it out. "Well? Are you going to tell me who it is, or what?"

"You know Kip Carmichael?"

"Yes."

"He's taking me." Or I'm taking him. Whichever.

"Sasquatch is your date?"

"Yes."

If sarcasm could form a laugh, Mariah pulls it off. "A guy named Sasquatch is taking you to your engineering banquet. Nice one, Teddy. Way to raise your expectations."

The applicator wand of black mascara pauses over my lashes. "What's that supposed to mean?"

No one has anything bad to say about Kip, other than a few guys who think he's an asshole—so I don't know why Mariah has that look of disgust on her face.

Or is it something else?

"You sound…" Jealous. *Bitter.* "Petty."

"I'm not being petty. Like I care who your date it. It's one night; it's not like you're actually *dating* the guy."

I say nothing, instead, resume my primp session by uncapping a tube of mauve lip tint.

"Unless you are." She's standing up straight now, arms crossed, a slight glare across her brow. "Are you dating him, Teddy?"

"I think that's what I'd call it, yeah. I'm dating him."

"Since when?"

"Since..." I count back a few weekends, trying to figure out the timeline. "A few weeks."

"A few weeks! What the hell, why didn't you say anything?"

I laugh, careful not to smudge my lipstick. "Why didn't I *say* anything? Are you serious? You haven't noticed I haven't been home the past three weekends? I could have been dead somewhere—you never even text me anymore."

"If I had known you were screwing Kip Carmichael, I probably would have been more worried."

I turn to face her, aghast. "And why is that?"

"Because. He's deplorable."

Deplorable? I laugh again. "I can't believe you right now. What do you have to be jealous of?"

"Don't be ridiculous."

"Then why would you say that about my boyfriend?"

"So he's your boyfriend now?" Mariah's own laugher comes out cold. "Two seconds ago you were just *dating*."

"Who are you?" I whisper. "I have done nothing but be a good friend. This entire year, you've been horrible—

honestly, Mariah, you care more about parties and guys than you do about me."

"That's not true."

"Isn't it?"

"No."

"Liar." I'm grateful for these heels when I stand at my full height—grateful for the added inches, so my room-mate and I see eye-to-eye. "Tessa and Cameron are always happy for me. They lent me these clothes." My hands sweep down my body, over the fabric of my dress. "They offered to come help me get dressed. You? Said you were busy, and you're not doing anything but watching TV."

"I have homework," she argues.

"It's Saturday. Since when do you study on the week-end?" The answer is never. "And how many times have I dropped everything for you? To help you. To do your makeup, or borrow a car so *I* can drive us places, or spot *you* money—money I do not have—for something when I'm broke. I always find a way, Mariah. Always. You never do the same for me anymore." I take a breath. "I don't know what I did to make you resent me, but I'm sick of your shitty attitude."

There. I said it.

"Wow, Farmer Ted—tell me how you *really* feel."

My nostrils flare at the moniker I hate so much; neck bristles. She knows I hate it and used it on purpose.

"I just did."

We glare at each other, in the small bathroom of our apartment, but something in her gaze—the way she's watching me a bit warily gives me pause.

Softens my stance a little.

I cock my head, waiting—because I know there's something she wants to say.

"Everything is so easy for you." Mariah says it slowly, in a low tone of voice.

It's not what I'm expecting her to say, not at all.

"Are you insane?" I blurt, damn certain my eyes are bugging out of my skull. "Nothing comes easy for me. What are you talking about?"

Her eyes go wide too. "Are you kidding? Why does everything work out for you? I fuck everything up and you always come out smelling like roses."

What the hell is she going on about? "You're confusing me, Mariah."

How is this girl jealous of me?

My mother works two jobs, and we've lived above a bar most of my life. I have a grant, which means I won't have to get another job this semester, but it wasn't always that way. For three years I've gone to school and worked, never having time off. I have to buy all my clothes discounted, or borrow them from friends.

I'm not sexy, or glamourous, or tall—like her.

Her parents are still married; her dad never ran out on her mom. Middle class, hard-working, and supportive, Mariah never wanted for anything.

What the hell is she resentful of me for?

"I'm flunking out, okay? My grades suck and I got put on academic probation at the end of last year—I thought I would raise them and not have to tell anyone, but that hasn't happened. I'm still below a two point oh."

Far be it from me to point out the fact that if she did more studying than partying, she might not be in this predicament.

"My parents always thought living with you would help my study habits, but obviously it hasn't." Her laugh is rueful. "I'll probably have to move home and go to Community College— if I even get accepted." She blows out a sigh, fingers tugging at the bun in her hair. "I have no love life. Guys are assholes, and none of them text back when they say they're going to—and here you have this awesome, *popular* guy chasing after you. You got this grant, so you can at least afford the next year of tuition, and—"

"What does this have to do with me?" I interrupt, still not following. "Because it sounds like you're blaming your problems on me, and I have zero to do with any of them."

I refuse to be anyone's scapegoat.

She ignores my question, continuing the pity party she's invited me to. "I thought I could handle casual sex, but that isn't working out for me either. I want…I'm sick of feeling used."

"Then maybe you should stop sleeping with a new guy every weekend." It slips out before I can stop myself and four eyes widen from surprise—hers and mine.

Oops.

"How do you know I've slept with a different guy every weekend?"

"I don't?"

"Let me guess; Kip told you."

My silence speaks volumes.

"How nice for you. Gossip from Jock Row."

"We don't sit and gossip about you. He just mentioned it once."

Mariah's face is an unflattering shade of red, from her cheeks to the tips of her ears.

"This all started before I met Kip, Mariah. You can be jealous or blame me for what's going on, but we both know none of this has anything to do with me." My hands are on my hips, confrontationally. "If you don't show me some respect, I'm moving out at semester—if you're not suspended first."

I brush past her, satisfied to have shocked her.

For the first time in our friendship, I've got the upper hand—and I'm keeping it.

Kip will be so proud of me.

***

I'm outside my apartment waiting for Kip; it's warm enough tonight that I won't freeze while I stand here—certainly not as cold as his house was the night his furnace went out. The memory puts a smile on my lips and I press a hand to my lower stomach.

Ugh. These butterflies…

My heart is still beating wildly from my argument with Mariah; I can't believe it took me so long to stand up to her. It actually felt incredible—a giant weight lifted off my shoulder that I finally said what I've been wanting to say—provoked by the fact that she couldn't have cared less that I was going out, didn't offer to help get me ready though I've spent countless hours doing *her* hair and makeup in the past, like her personal stylist.

All she would have had to do was offer to help.

So easy. So simple.

The past few weeks have really opened my eyes to what kind of friend she has become. It makes me sad to know we've grown so far apart that I no longer trust her, but at the same time, I'm excited about the new friends I've been making lately. I have more in common with Renee and Miranda, two girls I *just* met yet and have been getting calls and texts from all week, and they even made a spot for me today at Kip's game.

I have more in common with them than I do with the person I've spent the past three years living with.

I finally see that now.

My heels click on the pavement as I impatiently re-adjust my stance, the strappy leather shoes another loan from Cameron. The dress is also, a short, aqua blue shift with white trim and embroidered white flowers around the halter neckline.

I feel cute. Pretty.

Can't quite quell the nerves bombarding me as I stand here, impatiently waiting on Kip.

This will be our first date.

The first time he's going to see me really dressed up, wearing high heels and a fancy dress.

I fiddle with the gold hoop in my ear, glancing up when a tall, blond guy begins a steady stroll up the sidewalk to my apartment complex, heart racing a little when his face comes into the light.

He's so handsome I dip my head, embarrassed to look directly at him, afraid I'll get caught ogling, especially when I'm waiting on someone else.

Dark jeans. Brown dress shoes that shine under the lights. Baby blue polo shirt under a dark leather jacket.

I step aside so he can pass, brushing back my hair to busy my hands, tucking my purse more securely under my armpit.

And there go those damn butterflies.

Only…

He doesn't pass by me.

He stops.

Reaches down and puts his hands on my shoulders, leaning in and, "Oh my god, what the hell do you think you're doing!"

Yes, I realize I'm shouting, but that's what you're supposed to do when you're assaulted on a sidewalk in front of your own damn home.

"Get your hands off me!"

"Teddy, calm down," the hot guy's voice instructs.

But I don't calm down—I elbow him in the gut.

"*Oof.* Relax babe," the guy croaks out, slightly bent at the waist. "It's me. Relax, it's me."

Me *who*?

"I'm calling campus security. And…and I have a—a boyfriend you know, a really big one. He's *huge*, and he's going to kick your *ass* when he gets here. He'll be here any minute."

"God you're cute when you're threatening to kick my ass."

That voice.

That laugh.

Oh.

My.

God.

"*Kip?*"

That handsome face contorts, amused. And so handsome. "Who the hell did you think I was?"

"A rapist."

"Do I look like a rapist to you?" I'm so intent on studying him, I can't tell if he's being sarcastic or not.

He looks *hot*. He *is* hot. Like—there are no words for it. He's clean shaven, and his hair has been trimmed into way too trendy of a cut, short on the sides and longer on the top, combed back and styled—expensively.

Where do they even have salons around here that can cut a guy's hair like that?

Kip spins in circle on the heel of his highly polished leather shoes and wipes a hand across his smooth, freshly shaven chin.

There's a cleft there, and a slight dimple in his cheek.

Sweet mother of all that is holy.

"What do you think?" He spans his arms wide, inviting me to give him a once-over.

"I—I…I don't know what I think."

"What do you mean you don't know?" The poor guy looks genuinely confused, while I…am genuinely confused.

"Why did you do this?" I can't stop myself from asking.

"What kind of question is that? I did it for you."

"For *me*? Why?"

"Help me out here for a minute, Teddy. We're going somewhere nice, so you can receive an award—did you really want to show up with a dude they call Sasquatch, or did you want to show up with someone who looks respectable?"

Respectable is an understatement. Kip looks classy, refined, and *out of my league.*

I hate that I'm feeling this way; it's not his fault. It's my insecurities.

Shocking me like this certainly did not help, though, not when the banquet begins in less than an hour.

How am I supposed to sit next to him at the dinner table without staring? I won't be able to help myself; it will be like trying to ignore an exotic animal that's right beside you, purring.

"Why would you do this to me tonight?" I blurt out, unable to stop myself.

Kip looks stunned. "*Do* this to you? I don't get it—what did I do?"

"This." I gesture wildly. "The hair. The beard."

"I shaved? Got a haircut? For you?" He's staring down at me like I've grown three heads.

"Right before my banquet? How am I supposed to concentrate now?" I grip my purse and throw my hands up, frustrated—mostly with myself and my reaction to the situation. "I'm so freaked out right now, Kip, I don't even know what to do with myself."

He tries to put his hands on me again, resting those big, beautiful palms on my bare shoulders. "Babe, it's me.

Just…different."

Oh god, he just called me babe—sensory and emotional overload.

"Different? It's different, all right. God, Kip. I can't even look you in the eyes right now."

They look clear, deeper and richer than they've ever been, shining down at me. Baffled.

Hurt.

Irritated.

"Don't you think you're overreacting just a little bit? Most girls would be happy their…person shaved. My sister said you'd be thrilled."

I am one hundred percent overreacting, but knowing that isn't stopping my mouth from saying things I shouldn't be saying in tones that shouldn't leave my lips.

"I didn't fall for *this* guy. I fell for the *other* guy. This is too much for me. I'm sorry if I'm being weird, but—you have to cut me some slack here. You completely ambushed me."

"I cut my hair and shaved." He's not impressed with my argument, tone flat. "I didn't dye my beard pink and get a tattoo, for fuc—" Kip takes a deep breath, hands digging deep into the pockets of his jacket. "Do you not want me to go with you, Teddy?"

I suddenly feel like the biggest bitch on the face of the planet, making him feel like total shit because of the way he looks. He looks nice—that's my issue? That he looks too handsome? That he's *too* good-looking?

Apparently, I need therapy, not a boyfriend.

Jesus, Teddy, get a grip.

"I know I'm being unreasonable, and I'm...sorry." I steady my breath. "I'm sorry."

His arms go around my waist, pulling me in. "Don't worry about it. Let's just go and have a good time tonight, yeah?" Kip smells divine, his smooth jawline skimming mine, nuzzling my cheek, rubbing up and down. "Feels good, doesn't it?" his hypnotic voice murmurs.

God, it *does*. It feels orgasmic.

I go to my tiptoes, eyes fluttering closed as aftershave, freshly shaved skin, and his warm breath assail me all at once.

But I feel like I'm hugging a stranger.

And I wonder if I'll get over it before I *ruin* everything.

***

KIP

Teddy has been acting weird all fucking night, and it's starting to piss me off.

I've never had this problem with a girl before, never had one keep me at arm's length because of the way I look.

How fucked up is that?

If I was butt ugly, it would be one thing. But I'm not.

Girls have been chasing me around, trying to trap me into relationships since adolescence, and the one girl I finally decide to let catch me?

Treats me like a fucking pariah.

I thought she'd be happy, for fuck's sake, not act like I betrayed her by being attractive.

Agitated, my leg bounces under the table, the high-end

denim suffocating me, stiff because I haven't worn it in yet. My shoes pinch, and the collar around my neck chokes.

I did this for her, and she's acting like I committed a crime.

It's just. A fucking. Haircut.

Come on—am I that unrecognizable without the beard?

It did occur to me when I watched the stubble rinse down the drain that I look incredibly different, but it didn't occur to me that Teddy wouldn't like it.

It didn't occur to me that she liked me just fine the way I was.

Preferred it, apparently.

Kind of fucked up, if you ask me, considering I looked like a goddamn mountain man—on a good day. Or Paul Bunyan or Grizzly Adams or whoever it was she likes to call me.

She's said so herself dozens of times.

I wouldn't say she's ignoring me now, not exactly— but she's not looking directly at me, either.

And I'm not sure what to fucking do with myself.

So.

While she's talking to the girl next to her—some girl named Jenna who squealed and clapped like a damn lunatic when she won a trip to Florida as the raffle prize—I whip out my cell phone and message the one person who can help me sort this shit out.

Me: SOS

Ronnie: *What did you do this time?*

Me: *Teddy isn't a fan of the shaved look. What the hell*

do I do now?

Ronnie: *WHAT DO YOU MEAN SHE ISN'T A FAN?
Is she BLIND?? Does she not SEE you?*

Me: *Okay, first of all, stop shouting. Secondly, no.
Pretty sure she liked it before when I looked homeless.*

Ronnie: *Well she's just going to have to get over it,
isn't she?*

Me: *But WHAT DO I DO?*

Ronnie: *I don't know KIPLING—you can't go to the
bathroom and grow it all back, you idiot.*

Me: *You're the one who TOLD ME TO SHAVE and
now my girlfriend won't even look at me.*

Ronnie: *Do not blame this on me you little shithead.
You shouldn't have listened.*

Ronnie: *Wait. Back up. She's your GIRLfriend now?
Since when? You've been dating for like, five minutes.*

Me: *I don't have time to argue with you about seman-
tics, VeRONica.*

My fingers brutally attack the screen of my phone,
pounding out word after furious word in reply. Why is
Ronnie like this? Why can't she just tell me what to freaking do?

"Who ya texting?" Teddy's sweet voice interrupts,
eyes wide. I can tell she's trying to be civil and excited.
"You look so angry."

That's one way of putting it. "My sister. She's the one
who told me to shave my face and cut my hair, so I'm
chewing her ass out."

"Kip…" She looks so full of regret. And sad.

And I can't, for the life of me, figure out why.

Up front, professors and department heads are taking seats in the chairs lining the stage. A technician plugs in and taps on the microphone, testing it for sound. Taps once, twice, the echo filling the cavernous room.

"Looks like they're ready to get started. We can talk about this later."

I face the front, presenting her with my profile.

My chiseled, flawless profile, jaw set rigidly.

The one she apparently can't stand to look at without all the scruff.

Gag, right? So fucked up.

"Right," I hear her murmur, hand fidgeting atop the cream linen tablecloth. We're done with dinner, the usual university cuisine when they're feeding students on the cheap: chicken breast, mashed potatoes, shitty gravy, and a vegetable medley. Brownie for dessert, none of it worth whatever she paid for the tickets.

But.

Whatthe*fuck*ever.

Goddamn I'm pissed.

My leg continues to bounce under the table, and if Teddy can feel the vibration from it, she isn't going to say anything. I give her a fake, toothy smile when she glances over, notecards in her hand bearing the short speech she prepared.

It's another ten minutes before they call her name; six students go before her, each of them receiving an award, scholarship, or honor from the university.

Then.

"Theodora Grace Johnson, receiving the William Richards Fellowship Grant."

The audience applauds politely as Teddy stands. Hesitates at my side before leaning over and softly kissing my cheek. The spot tingles even after she walks toward the stage, and I touch it with my forefinger—it's sticky from her lip gloss, and when I lower my arm and look at my hand, I see the light pink stain.

Okay, *fine*.

Maybe I won't be that pissed off later.

I'll get over it.

Teddy is shaking some dean's hand, smiling—beaming, actually—before taking the mic and thanking the crowd.

"Thank you Doctor Langford." She clears her throat. "And thank you to the William Richards trust committee for choosing me as this year's recipient." She clears her throat again before nervously chuckling. "Um…things haven't always been easy for me. My mother raised me by herself, and I was alone a lot while she worked. This grant is going to make a huge difference for me this year, and it will allow me to do what I love: discover and help develop the cities in which we live." She glances up from her small, white notecards. "I also want to say…I'm thankful for my new friends."

I sit up straighter in my chair. She means me, right? I'm one of her new friends, albeit one who likes to get naked with her. I count, yeah?

"And Kip, thank you for…everything."

Wait. What?

That's it?

That's the end of her speech? *Thank you for every-thing?* Am I supposed to know what that means?

Thanks for the orgasm. Thanks for sucking on my tits. Thanks for keeping an eye on me at parties?

That wasn't a goodbye thank you, was it? Shit, what if it was? It did sound kind of ominous. Or maybe I'm reading into it too much.

My eyes never leave her as she weaves her way back to the table, smiling and saying hello to people along the way, and I stand to pull her chair out before she sits back down.

She faces the stage, presenting me with the back of her head, and I want nothing more than to lean over and kiss her smooth, pale shoulder.

We sit through another ten speeches, which—miserably—takes over an hour, the button on my shirt screaming to come undone.

Spend another few minutes in the car on our way back to her apartment. The silence is almost deafening and ridiculous and so uncalled for I can't stop the bitter laugh rising from my chest.

"What's so funny?" Teddy asks, signed grant check clasped in her fingers protectively.

"Nothing. This is just so fucking stupid, that's all." I put my car in park, turning to face her, arm resting on the steering wheel. "Why are you acting like this? I haven't done anything."

"I guess—I don't know. I know I'm being weird, okay?"

"Actually, it's not okay, Teddy."

She ruined a perfectly good evening, one I looked forward to all week.

"Everything was great this morning, and now you've done a complete turnaround." She came to my game, sat with Renee, Miranda, and another teammate's girlfriend, cheered for me the entire time and patched me up afterward.

We went for lunch before I dropped her off at home then I went for my haircut and shaved and—

"That was before I knew what you looked like." Her voice is small, coming from the dark recesses of my SUV.

"I'm sorry, what? That sounds like an insult. And since when is it a bad thing for a guy to be attractive?"

"It's not. This isn't about your face."

Could have fooled me. "Then what is it about?"

"I honestly have no idea."

"Okay, so what now? What do we do? I can grow the beard back, Teddy—I can grow it back starting tomorrow."

"But I already know what you look like."

"Jesus, Teddy, why are you making this such a big deal?" I can't stop my voice from rising.

Hers rises, too. "I don't know Kip! I don't...know. Honestly, I loved the way you looked before."

"Honestly, Teddy, I loved the way you didn't judge me before."

"Ouch."

"Yeah, well, the truth hurts, doesn't it?"

I regret the words as soon as I say them because they come out harsh, and rude, and bitter.

I soften my attitude. "Come home with me. Please.

That's the only way we're going to get past this."

Let me change your mind.

Every nerve in my body screams that she's going to say no. She's going to reject the idea, hop out of my car, and I'm never going to see her again.

"Yes. You're right."

I let out a breath, a puff of air, then clutch the steering wheel with both hands. "All right then. Great."

I'm so fucking relieved.

Putting the vehicle in reverse, I take us back the way we came. Past the administration buildings. The student union and library. Away from campus and three miles out of town.

Only when we're sitting cross-legged on the living room floor does Teddy speak again.

"I think…I reacted so badly because…the differences between us suddenly became so pronounced. You came strutting toward me looking so handsome and fancy, and I was standing there wearing a borrowed dress and borrowed shoes. I borrow a car—I have nothing."

"That doesn't matter to me." I say it with conviction. "And I don't strut."

She laughs, stretching out her leg toward me. I take her foot in my lap and begin massaging her pretty ankle as she talks. "But it matters to *me*; the way we were raised and the roads we're taking, you know? It became so very clear to me after I realized it was you."

"I can't help the fact that my parents are wealthy, Teddy. You can't hold that against me—people have been doing it my whole life. It's a hard thing to escape. That's why

I came here."

"I know. I get judged too, for being poor, and I *hate* that. I'm not saying it was horrible being me, but my mother works in a bar—and not a very nice one. A few times we've lived above it, and it was loud and smoky, and I'm never living like that again. That's why I'm busting my ass now."

"I don't think we've talked about this, but...I'll probably work for my dad when I graduate. Is that going to be a problem?"

"That's not my decision—why would you ask me that?"

"Uh, because you're my girlfriend?"

"I am?"

How did she not know that? "Affirmative. And you probably won't be able to get rid of me."

"Oh." She bites down on her bottom lip, pleased. "Well in that case, you should probably take me upstairs."

She doesn't have to tell me twice.

I stand, bending at the waist and scooping her up as if she weighs nothing—she doesn't—and carry her up the stairs. Over the threshold to my bedroom, setting her on the edge of the bed.

"I don't think I got the chance to tell you how pretty you look tonight."

Blue is a great color on her; the dress is prim but sexy, both hugging her curves and hiding them at the same time. Her toned arms and legs are the only skin showing, but when she slides off the bed to stand on the floor and presents me with her back, I get to see more of her as I slide the zipper all the way down.

It whirs, causing both of us to shiver when it splits.

Smooth skin.

No bra.

Sensible cotton underwear.

No frills for my girl, but that will come in time; when she trusts me and doesn't get freaked out by expensive gifts, I'm going to spoil the shit out of her. Buy her lacey bras and panties and whatever the hell she wants.

"God this is taking you forever," she complains when I still haven't slid the dress off her body.

"Patience."

My hands are *huge* compared to her shoulders, and I love watching them glide across her skin. Love the way she feels under my callused palms—have from the first time I touched her.

Knew she would feel this way the second I saw her standing at that keg in the living room of the rugby house.

Hell, I think I fucking loved her the second I saw her. Period.

When you know, you'll know, my obnoxious sister is always telling me about finding the right girl for me, never really believing I'd sworn off of them forever.

Dammit. I *hate* when she's right.

It's so fucking annoying.

She's definitely going to be rubbing this one in my face when I see her.

I finally get Teddy naked, hoist her onto the bed, propping her ass on the edge. Spread her legs and kneel.

"Oh my god, what are you doing?" She's raised up, trying to see what it is I'm doing.

"Shh. I'm gonna show you what it's like to have a smooth face between your legs before I grow it back. No beard burn."

"Uh-h o-okay," she stutters, letting her head hit the mattress, her feet now propped on my shoulders like stirrups at the goddamn gyno's office.

I chuckle to myself at the reference then focus on the task in front of me.

Man she has a gorgeous pussy. It's not waxed like most girls are doing these days; it's trimmed and short, with a pretty strip running up the center. She keeps the sides nice and smooth, and I show my appreciation by licking one side then the other.

I press two fingers inside, licking her up the middle—she loves when I do that, squirms and sighs and gasps.

Wiggles her hips and thrashes her head when I bear down, sucking her clit.

She tastes fucking incredible, like sex and orgasms. And she's mine.

So sweet and kind.

Shy but doesn't shy away from telling me how she feels.

It doesn't take long for me to make her come; her lower half convulses within minutes, the shockwaves of pleasure causing her to moan my name.

Reaches for me, pulls me up onto the bed.

We lie facing each other, her kisses on my wet mouth a total turn-on; I know she can taste herself on my lips, and that turns me on too.

Delicate fingers stroke the side of my face as she regards me, lying on her side. Her fingertip trails along my eyebrow, down my smooth cheek, and along the square jawline I could only hide with two years of beard growth.

"You're so handsome," Teddy says at last, a small smile playing on her lips. "Pretty boy."

"I'm no pretty boy."

Now her smile is rueful. "No, you're not, are you?"

"I'm a mountain man, remember?"

She rolls her beautiful eyes. "You haven't even been camping."

"And I suppose you're going to take me?"

A laugh. "Hell no! I'm terrible at camping—although it might be worth it to see you in the woods. Do you even know how to build a bonfire?"

"Hey, don't make fun of me. It's not my fault I've never slept in the damn woods—my parents wouldn't know the first thing about roughing it." A thought strikes me. "Bet my sister would go with us. She's up for anything."

Teddy's hand flattens over my abs, working its way down my body. "Did you tell her about what happened tonight? How I freaked out?"

"Yeah."

"What did she say?"

"That I never should have taken her advice and shaved my beard off."

My girlfriend laughs, boobs jiggling. "I don't know about *that*—she's been right about a *few* things. Just give a girl a little warning next time you clean up, would ya?"

TWO MONTHS LATER

"The Epilogue and the moment I've been waiting for..."

KIP

No warning was necessary, because the beard is back—not as thick as it once was, but it will get there.

I'm keeping my hair the same—shaved short on the sides and longer on the top—because quite frankly, with my bushy beard growing in, I'm kind of rocking the Viking look and it's fucking badass.

No one will be messing with me any time soon.

"Babe, did you see the stuff my mom left for you in the kitchen?" My parents were just here visiting; once they heard I had a girlfriend, they didn't hesitate to fly out to meet her from whatever city they've been staying in.

"No, I haven't. What has she done now?"

My mother immediately took to Teddy, and in the two months since we officially started dating, she has already begun mentally planning a wedding. I don't know how I feel about my mom's meddling, considering Teddy and I haven't even had sex yet, but there's nothing I can do.

I go with it.

"Had some clothes sent I think, sweaters and stuff from the department store—she said to keep what you want and send back what you don't."

"What? Why would she do that?"

"Because that's what Lilian Carmichael does." I take a stack of folded clothes, brand new with tags, off the counter and hold them up. "See? These are for me. Half of them are too small."

My mom still doesn't get that I'm six foot four and don't wear a size large—haven't since I was a freshman in high school.

"She can't help herself, babe." I apologize. "I'm sorry."

"Don't apologize—it's so thoughtful. I'll have to send her a thank you text."

Between my mother and sister, the three of them have this weird group text where they send memes and jokes back and forth almost every day—most of them at my expense. Har har.

Whatever. I'm just glad my family likes her.

I wasn't sure how dating her would go over with my parents at first—she doesn't come from money and she has no pedigree. But as it turns out, my parents are just uptight and not complete assholes. They want me to be happy, and I won't lie and say it wouldn't have mattered if they didn't like Teddy.

Because it would have.

Teddy plans to move in with me at the end of the semester, out of her apartment with Mariah and into my house.

It makes sense, since:

1. She's always at my place anyway.

2. Mariah hasn't been able to get her grades up and will probably be transferring to community college.

3. The two of them couldn't have grown apart any more than they have and it's put a huge strain on their friendship, so Teddy would have moved out anyway.

4. She is always at my place anyway.

My parents totally support her moving in, and Teddy's mom has been awesome too, glad her daughter will be struggling a lot less.

"Do you know what your sister sent me?"

Shit. My sister is becoming worse than my mother, sending ridiculous gifts, notes, and stupid shit Teddy is never going to use. Like inappropriate stationary, T-shirts with quotes on them, and gold bracelets—with profanity.

"Do I really want to know?"

"Actually, I think you do." She slowly lifts the hem of a pink shirt that says *Spread kindness like confetti*. Out peeks a bit of red lace that covers her entire stomach.

"Uh…what is *that*?"

"It's a teddy." She laughs. "Get it?"

Yes, I get it.

"My sister sent you lingerie? What the hell is wrong with her?"

"It's a teddy, Kip. A *teddy*?" She stares at me, waiting for it to sink in, but I'm slow. "Surely you haven't been knocked on the head that much."

She goes for the fly of her jeans, unbuttoning them slowly, then pushes the denim down her slim hips. Turns and heads toward the stairs, red lace thong nestled neatly between two very sexy ass cheeks.

A teddy.

"Oohhh…"

She shoots me a wink over her shoulder, hips swaying, palm sliding up the shiny bannister. Long hair swishing across her shoulders with every movement.

When she reaches the top, she turns, lifting the T-shirt and pulling it all the way off.

"Holy shit."

I waste no time, taking the stairs two at a time, and my girlfriend squeals, racing for the bedroom.

She's on top of the bed, on her knees by the time I get there, both of us out of breath and laughing.

"You are so slow," she jokes. "And I don't mean how long it took you to get up here."

"My sister is a pervert, sending you underwear."

She runs a finger along one of the satin straps, toying with me. "I think it's clever."

"Still, she shouldn't be sending my girlfriend skimpy shit." I sound like a disgruntled toddler.

"Really Kip? You choose now to turn into a prude?"

"My family is so far up our asses I can't even see straight anymore."

"Stop pouting and come kiss me."

Climbing up onto the bed, I'm on my knees too, hands sliding up her bare arms to her shoulders. I hook my thumbs under the strap of the lingerie, tugging it down.

Palm her breasts, the pads of my fingers gently rolling over her firm nipples.

"I think I'm ready," she moans, head tipping back.

I kiss the tender skin there, careful not to mar it with the stubble of my beard. "Ready for what, babe?"

"To have sex." Teddy rolls her eyes.

We've been waiting—two months I've waited for her to say she's ready, never rushing or pressuring her but wanting to fuck her all the same.

"My condoms are like, a hundred years old."

"Then it's a good thing I'm on the pill."

Say what now? "When did you do that?"

"Last month. I went to health services just to be safe—just in case."

"You mean I get to bone you bareback?"

"Um…yes?"

Sweet!

I've almost never been this excited in my entire fucking life. "I've been training for this moment."

Teddy laughs, a high-pitched giggle of nerves. "Would you knock it off?"

"Nope, can't—too excited."

"You're supposed to be quiet and serious."

"Why? I want to be loud and bang the headboard into the wall." I hop a little on the bed to illustrate my point, bouncing Teddy's tits in the process.

Win-win.

"You are not banging me into any headboards." The sassy little brat shoves my arm before flopping onto her back and throwing her arms behind her head. "You can get me naked, though, if you want."

I want.

And I do.

My dick is so stiff and hard it's painful and becoming unbearable.

I get to have sex with my girlfriend.

I am having *sex*, motherfuckers!

I try to curb my enthusiasm, but it's hard.

Really hard.

I grin at my own pun, even though I didn't say it out loud, and as if Teddy can read my mind, she rolls her eyes up at me as I shuck my shirt, pants, and—

"Can you take off your socks?"

And socks.

If I wasn't so damn horny, I'd be nervous too—getting blowjobs and jerking off is fine, but nothing beats the real deal. Not when all five foot five of beautiful, funny, and intelligent sleeps in bed next to you every night, reminding you.

It's to the point where every one of Teddy's quiet sighs and inhaled breaths gets me hard. Every flirty laugh and touch to my body.

I lean in, kissing the tip of her breast through the sheer, red fabric of her lingerie—her teddy—wetting it through the lace.

Kiss along her collarbone, the column of her neck.

We kiss, making out—tongues wet, mouths greedy—as my hands roam her body, feeling for the snaps at the crotch of her bodysuit.

Rub her pussy with my thumb until her pelvis begins rocking and she squirms.

Until she begs me to, "Take it off."

Then I'm above her, teasing her clit with the head of my cock, guiding it along her slit, stroking up and down, watching as her pupils dilate and nostrils flare. This is different than when we dry hump—this is the moment we both know we're going to fuck.

Screw.

Make love. Whatever you want to call it, I'm ready.

We both are.

"Go slow," comes her soft request.

"Scared?" I kiss her forehead and brush away a few strands of hair.

"A little." Her hands cuff my biceps, and she's biting down on her lower lip.

"Me too."

"You are? Why?"

"I've never done this with anyone I gave a shit about before."

"And you give a shit about me, huh?" Her eyes are sparkling, pleased.

She knows what I mean—that I fucking love her even if neither of us has said the words out loud to each other yet.

We know.

I move again, this time pushing forward, cringing. Calling on my self-control—I have tons of it, I do; it's just so fucking hard not to go balls deep.

She's wet so my cock glides in easy, searching for that point of resistance we're *both* dreading.

I kiss her again, catching the gasp that escapes her lungs, pausing before going farther.

"Should I stop?" The last thing I want to do is hurt her.

"No. Let's get it over with." When I laugh, she smacks me on the arm. "Stop it—your whole body is vibrating."

"Right. Game faces." I stop laughing.

Time to get serious.

"Just do it, okay? The longer it takes you the worse it's going to be."

"Are you sure?" I'm doubtful.

"No, but it's only going to hurt this one time, right?"

"How the hell should *I* know?" It certainly didn't hurt when I lost *my* virginity—it felt so fucking good, I came within seconds.

"Push, Kip."

Push.

Oh fuck she's tight. And wet and…tight.

She tenses beneath me when I thrust all the way in, expecting the worst, eyes squeezing shut.

One peeps open. "Was that it?"

"I mean…we're not done, if that's what you mean."

"No, I mean—that pinched but it didn't really hurt. Is that normal?"

Again, how the hell would I know? "Not sure babe. Can I move now?"

Her only reply is a wiggle of her hips, and I begin moving, in and out, thrusting slowly. Gradually going faster, gauging her reaction by reading her face.

Mouth gaped open, her expression is almost unreadable.

Hmm.

Bracing myself with one elbow, I reach between our bodies, thumb finding her nub. Her clit. That tiny spot in her pussy I know will make her come.

I rub.

Slow circles as I fuck her slowly, around and around and around...

So wet.

So tight.

My forehead perspires, and Jesus, I wish it fucking wouldn't because who wants to be covered in sweat while they're banging their girlfriend for the first time?

Not me.

Christ.

But...

Teddy begins moaning.

Low in her throat. Tiny gasps.

Holy shit, is she going to...?

Is she seriously about to fucking come?

There is no way.

She is.

She does.

"Oh my *god*, Kip, oh my g-god, oh my god, *oh my god…*"

The clenching of her inner muscles and ripples of pleasure send shocks to my dick, my balls receiving the message of *all clear.*

"*Fuck*," I moan into her hair. "Oh fuck, Teddy."

When I roll off of her, I take her hand in mine and hold it while we both stare at the ceiling, waiting to catch our breath.

***

"I cannot believe you actually had an orgasm." Honestly. Still can't fucking believe it. The odds of that happening were slim to none. I didn't think virgins could orgasm their first time.

"Neither can I."

"I must have a magic cock or something." What other explanation could there possibly be?

"Let's not get ahead of ourselves, okay? If you hadn't been rubbing me off at the same time, no *way* would I have come."

"Wanna make a bet?" My dick becomes alert, interested in the conversation.

"Kip, I am not having sex with you again tonight." Even in the dark, I can hear her eyes roll. "I'll barely be able to walk to the bathroom as it is."

"Fine, but if you change your mind, I'll be over here, thinkin' 'bout that sex."

"Keep your hands to yourself, unless you want to cuddle me."

"Cuddling I can do. You want to be the big spoon or the little spoon?"

"Little spoon, please." Her small body fits itself into mine, ass against my cock, back against my chest. Perfect fit. "Can you not drape your giant arm over my stomach? I won't be able to breathe if you do—it weighs a ton."

My phone pings on the nightstand.

I ignore it, obviously.

"Are you going to see who that is?"

We both *know* who it is, because I never receive texts from anyone but Teddy, my parents, and Veronica. Sometimes from one of the guys on the team, but rarely.

"I don't want to know what Ronnie wants at this hour of the night."

"Kip, it's ten o'clock."

"So?"

"That is not late, and she's an hour behind us. Besides, what if it's an emergency?"

I glance down at Teddy, speaking into the crown of her head. "Are you serious? Nothing is ever an emergency with my sister. She's texting because she's nosy."

Her spidey senses were probably tingling, and she knows I just got laid so she's texting to investigate.

On the opposite nightstand, Teddy's phone pings. "It's like she *knows*."

Yeah, she knows all right.

"Send her a Snap of the teddy on the floor with my dirty underwear—that will get her to leave us alone."

"Your sister?" Teddy cocks a brow. "She'd only screen-shot it and use it against you later."

True. "What she needs to do is mind her own business."

"That's funny, Veronica minding her own business." Teddy laughs. "In her own way, she kind of played match-maker."

I'm quiet for a few seconds, considering that. "Holy shit. You're right."

"I am?"

"Yes, and that made me throw up in my mouth a little."

Teddy gives me a poke in the ribs. "Find out what she wants."

I sigh, rolling toward the nightstand.

Ronnie: *I told you so.*

Me: *That's why you're texting me at 10 PM? To say I told you so?*

Ronnie: *Yes.*

Me: *Explain*

A few seconds later, a screenshot pops up—it's part of the conversation we had weeks ago, on the weekend I brought Teddy back to my place. When I said we were only friends.

Me: *She's just a friend. Barely even a friend.*

Ronnie: *Mark my words, Kipling: this isn't going to have the ending you think it will...*

"God I hate it when she's right. It's so fucking annoy-ing."

Teddy is reading the text over my shoulder, and I can

feel her smiling against my skin, her hand stroking my back. Lips kissing my shoulder.

"I love that," comes her timid whisper. "And I love you."

I set the phone back down, and, careful not to crush her, flip to my back. Find her lips and kiss her.

"I love you too, babe." Then, "Can we not tell Ronnie she was right?"

"I think she already knows."

Yeah, probably. But still.

"Did she send you anything else besides that red thing?"

Teddy demurs, tracing my right pec with the tip of her finger. "That's for me to know and you to find out."

ACKNOWLEDGMENTS

Confession: I love beards.

I don't know what took me so long to write a character who sported one—and I don't know why it took so many calendar days to actually write and complete this book. I started early summer; normally, it takes me about four months to write a full-length novel, but this summer was rough going, and this one took me a good six months.

Slow. Going.

Not my norm, but nothing about this summer was normal. Not for me, anyway.

So I have to thank everyone who was patient with me; the people who were there for me when things weren't great. When life wasn't easy. When the words wouldn't come, no matter how hard I tried.

You can't force it.

My assistant Christine isn't just my assistant. She's one of my best friends **holds back the tears** and one of the people I reply on the most. Not just for book related business, but for…my heart. I confide in her, trust her, and love her dearly. She's my rock. Support. The one constant I have in my life right now besides my beautiful daughter.

I couldn't have made it though the summer, or finish this book, without Christine cheerleading me on. I know this manuscript made her nervous; I know she didn't think it would be done on time. I know she was afraid to read it, LOL.

I love you, Christine.

Meghan Quinn—you're another one that carried me

this summer. I know I gave you more than a few heart palpitations and stressed you out; thank you for being patient, and kind, and wonderful. I probably didn't deserve any of it, but I'm grateful for it. You're a true, fast friend.

Thank you to my Beta Readers, Laurie Darter and Jennifer Bidwell. I wasn't sure I'd even have the chance to have anyone take a peek at it in advance, and I think I exhaled a huge sigh of relief when you both actually liked the book.

My editor Caitlyn Nelson, whom I had to email multiple times and push back my editing dates **awkward smile** I was so relieved to make my deadline.

My proofreaders Jennifer VanWyk and Karen Lawson.

Formatter, Alyssa Garcia with Uplifting Designs.

It takes a Village to publish a book, and I haven't even thanked half the people who touched this novel, helped with teasers, graphics, promo, feedback, social media… the list goes on and on.

I'm grateful for you all.

Xoxo

Sara

OTHER TITLES BY SARA

The Kiss and Make Up Series

Kissing in Cars

He Kissed Me First

A Kiss Like This

#ThreeLittleLies Series

Things Liars Say

Things Liars Hide

Things Liars Fake

How to Date a Douchebag Series

The Studying Hours

The Failing Hours

The Learning Hours

The Coaching Hours

Jock Hard Series

Swich Hitter

Jock Row

Jock Rule

For a complete updated list visit:

www.authorsaraney.com/books

ABOUT SARA

Sara Ney is the USA Today Bestselling Author of the How to Date a Douchebag series, and is best known for her sexy, laugh-out-loud New Adult romances. Among her favorite vices, she includes: iced latte's, historical architecture and well-placed sarcasm. She lives colorfully, collects vintage books, art, loves flea markets, and fancies herself British.

For more information about Sara Ney and her books, visit:

Facebook
www.facebook.com/saraneyauthor

Twitter
www.twitter.com/saraney

Website
www.authorsaraney.com

Instagram
www.instagram.com/saraneyauthor

Books + Main
bookandmainbites.com/users/38

Subscribe to Sara's Newsletter
www.subscribepage.com/saraney

Facebook Reader Group: Ney's Little Liars
www.facebook.com/groups/1065756456778840/

Printed in Great Britain
by Amazon

12623371R00154